Landon Snow

BOOK ONE

Landon Snow

and the Auctor's Riddle

R. K. MORTENSON

BARBOUR
PUBLISHING

ISBN 1-59310-881-8

All scripture quotations are taken from the King James Version of the Bible.

Cover and interior illustrations by Cory Godbey, Portland Studios.
    www.portlandstudios.com
Cover design by DogEared Design, llc.

Published by Barbour Publishing, Inc., P.O. Box 719, Uhrichsville, Ohio 44683
www.barbourbooks.com

Our mission is to publish and distribute inspirational products offering exceptional value and biblical encouragement to the masses.

Member of the
Evangelical Christian
Publishers Association

Printed in the United States of America.
5 4 3 2 1

Dedication

This is for my godsons:

Silas Poston
Luke Nelson
Caleb Camrud

May God bless you and your dreams.

Acknowledgments

THANKS TO
My wife, Betsy, for giving me a dream-stone.
My daughter, Kyra, for sparking joy.
My mom for loving words.
My dad (whom I miss) for sighting "a single bird on a solitary
   branch."
My siblings, Brenda, Jody, Brian, Barry, and Marcie—and
   their families—for love and support.
The Johnson clan and beyond for love and support.

Chapter One

The leaves were already turning color and beginning to fall when the Snow family made their trek from Minneapolis north to Button Up, Minnesota. Landon, who was about to turn eleven years old, especially looked forward to this trip for two reasons. Well, two and a half, really. One: he got to see his grandfather, Grandpa Karl, who told wonderful stories and loved books. Two: Grandpa Karl would take him and anyone else who was interested to visit the oldest and largest privately funded library in the state. This was the Button Up Library, known to locals as the BUL. And the half reason Landon liked to visit his grandparents? Grandma Alice and her cooking. Especially her lemon bars. Mm, they were good.

Landon had forgotten that his mother's SUV was in the shop getting fixed, so when his two younger sisters called for window seats as they raced past him to the car, he stood momentarily stunned. This meant he would be stuck between them in the backseat of their dad's small sedan. It also meant there would be no DVD movie to watch. Landon would have been happy looking at a book for the three-and-a-half-hour drive. Except for one reason: reading in the car gave him a terrible headache.

Landon sighed. This was going to be a long trip.

Holly sat on his left and looked out the window, providing occasional commentary regarding the passing outside scene. "That's the fourth Dairy Queen since we left the Cities," she said. "And there's a big silver water tower with. . .eight legs. Like an alien spaceship spider."

Holly's straight blond hair shifted back and forth as she switched her gaze. She was ten years old, too, not even a full year younger than Landon. For an agonizing three weeks and three days, she and Landon were the same age. Even though his hair was much redder than hers, some people asked if they were twins because they were about the same height. Holly liked to say, "Yes, except we were born 341 days apart." And then Landon would feel his face warm up to match his hair color. Thank goodness his birthday was tomorrow! He would be older than Holly again for the rest of the year.

Bridget was seven years old, and she was snoozing. Her head of dark ringlets lolled against Landon's right shoulder. "Snizzzz," she said, and then she made sounds like an oscillating bicycle pump. She fell asleep during any trip over ten minutes in the car. When they arrived at their destination, she would wake with a start and ask the same three questions. "What? What happened? Where am I?" And someone or everyone would respond, "Get out of the car, Bridget. We're here." Landon thought the reason Bridget slept so much was because she asked so many questions. Questions were tiring, he reasoned. Answers were energizing.

Landon liked to have reasons for everything. But he tried not to ask too many questions. Instead, he came up with reasons on his own. It felt good to explain things, at least to himself. If he knew the reason for something, he was happy. If not, he was uncomfortable. For instance, even though he would have preferred to sit by a window and even more than that would have liked to ride in his mom's SUV, he understood the reasons for his current situation. These were that his mom's car was in need of repair and he had been too slow in remembering to call for a window seat. The first reason wasn't due to anyone's fault, really. And he could only blame himself for the second.

The sky was just beginning to dim as the car slowed to turn off from the highway.

"Seventeen water towers and five Dairy Queens," reported Holly. She craned her neck to see past Landon and Bridget to the right. "Button Up. Population 897. But now with the five of us. . .902."

She grinned at Landon, and he decided the reason she was grinning was because she liked numbers and was good at math. He sighed contentedly as they eased down Main Street toward the town's one hanging stoplight, which was always blinking yellow. It never turned red or green, he thought, because cars didn't have to stop and then go. They merely slowed down a little and looked for pedestrians. It was fitting that they slowed down here anyway, because just beyond the pulsing light rose the wide stone steps that led to the Button Up Library.

Holly's elbow absently nudged Landon. Her hair was practically brushing his left cheek as she leaned close to look out the windshield. "Landon," she whispered, "there it is."

Though he'd visited the library many times, the sight of it still caused his heart to leap and his breathing to quicken. "I know," he said in a reverent hush. "The BUL." His body was reacting like this because he was *excited.* And he knew why he was excited. The library was a magical place. And he was going to visit it tomorrow with Grandpa Karl. Inside were more books than even Holly could count.

"It looks like the Parthenon in Greece," said Holly. "Or the Supreme Court in Washington, DC."

Of course his sister had never been to those places or actually seen those buildings. But Landon nodded anyway, his mouth hanging open. The library indeed looked as if it had fallen here by accident, landing in almost-the-middle-of-nowhere between Brainerd, Minnesota, and Canada, rather than in some majestic metropolis. "Ten white pillars," Landon said, beating his sister to the punch.

"And forty-two steps up from the sidewalk," she added quickly.

Landon tilted his head, bumping hers. How could she have counted them so fast? The steps were becoming hard to distinguish in the graying light.

"I counted last year when you guys were inside," she said, as if reading his mind. "Twenty-two steps and then the landing, and then twenty more. And at the top—"

"The portico," said Landon. He caught his dad's eyes in the rearview mirror. His dad was smiling.

"Very good. And what does 'portico' mean?"

"It's like a porch," said Landon. "From the Latin word *porticus.*"

His dad shook his head, but Landon could tell he was still smiling. Then his mom spoke. "We've got smart kids, honey. Words, numbers, and—"

"Slumbers," said Landon, gently nudging Bridget. His parents laughed, and Bridget snorted in her sleep.

They reached the end of the street, and as the car turned right, Landon and Holly turned their heads left to keep looking at the library grounds.

Lights were shining up at the building as well as at an American flag atop a high pole. A proud stone lion stood on either side of the steps. The lions were like grand bookends, although the angular lighting caused them to appear shadowy and almost gargoylelike. Between the middle pillars and below the high center peak of the roof, the glass double doors briefly reflected a glint of outside light. Then they were dark.

Holly turned from the window and settled into her seat

with a sigh. "One thousand crystals," she said as if speaking to herself. "I'd sure like to know how many are in each row."

Landon frowned at her. Then his face relaxed, and he knew the answer. She was thinking of the crystal chandelier that hung in the library's foyer. It was too high up to possibly count the crystals from the marble floor. And it was so glittery you'd become dizzy simply trying. But he and Holly knew there were a thousand teardrop crystals, because that's how many Grandpa Karl said there were.

Holly's elbow suddenly jabbed him in the ribs, shattering his thoughts of the chandelier. "Hey," she said, "I could try counting the rows tomorrow. I wonder if they have a tall ladder."

The mere thought of climbing a ladder to that height made Landon light-headed. He closed his eyes and shook his head. Then he noticed not Holly's elbow, but her hand softly patting his jacket. "What's this?" She was leaning close to his chest as if listening for something.

He remembered his drawing and immediately thrust his hand inside his jacket to protect it. His fingers found the crisp, folded edge of the construction paper. He was no artist, and he meant for no one to see his sketch other than Grandpa Karl, though Grandma Alice was sure to see it, too. Landon had made it just last night, as a kind of thank-you card for whatever birthday gift Grandpa and Grandma would give him. It wasn't actually a card but a drawing done in black marker on rough white paper.

With his free hand, Landon warded Holly's away. Not wanting to tell her what the paper actually was, he decided to have a little fun. "It's a map," he said furtively, "for buried treasure."

She paused, not sure whether to take him seriously or not. "Unh-uh," she said.

He nodded. "Uh-huh."

She cocked her head and squinted. "Where?"

"The library," he said. Immediately, he regretted it. But the words had slipped out before he could stop them. He felt his face growing warm.

Holly grimaced and pulled away. "That's gross," she said, "and not very respectful, Landon." She faced her window, and Landon felt his heart sink.

The reason Landon wished he had not said he had a map to buried treasure in the library was because there really was something buried beneath the floor. It was no secret at all but fairly obvious to anyone who visited. Right there in the entryway, directly below the hanging chandelier of a thousand crystals, stood a rather unusual sculpture of shiny black stone. It was the size and shape of an actual rowboat. But that's not all. In the boat's pointed prow was propped a large, open book, also cut from black stone. On the left-hand page of the book, chiseled and inlaid with gold, were the words BARTHOLOMEW G. BENNEFORD, followed by a space, and then FOUNDER: HOUSE OF KNOWLEDGE AND ADVENTURE. Engraved in the right-hand page were the dates of Bartholomew's birth and death and an epitaph:

> WITH WORMS THE FISH HE FED.
> WITH LOVE THE BOOKS HE READ.
> LONG LIVE THE MEMORY
> OF A TRUE BOOKWORM.

They turned left onto a tree-lined road that began to wind uphill. It was darker among the trees. As the road curved back and forth, the car's headlamps illuminated tree trunks first on one side and then on the other side.

"Almost there," his dad announced. Landon's spirits lifted as they climbed the hill. He had another reason to be excited now. He was about to see his grandparents.

At the top of the climb, the trees gave way to open grass. The first long driveway on the right led to Grandma and Grandpa Snow's house. Gravel began to plink beneath the car as soon as they turned into the drive. Ahead of them stood the house—a two-and-a-half-story frame that reminded Landon of the letter H with an A-shaped top.

The tires stopped crunching, and the gravel quit plinking. As soon as the engine was cut off, Bridget stirred. "What? What happened? Where am I?"

"Get out of the car, Bridget," they all said. "We're here."

Holly jumped out quick as a rabbit, leaving her door partway open. Cool air poured in. Landon looked at Bridget and smiled. She was moving slower than a sloth. Stretching and yawning and blinking around as if the world were brand new. Though she was sure to figure it out soon enough, Landon felt better just telling her. "We're at Grandma and Grandpa's. In Button Up."

Bridget's mouth opened wide, and she made a moaning sound that seemed to indicate she understood.

"Good," said Landon. He climbed happily out Holly's side and closed the door.

His grandparents had come out onto the porch to greet them. Everyone was hugging, and Landon sank into Grandma Alice and felt her arms encircle him. She felt and smelled doughy and powdery like a bakery, and Landon wondered if there were fresh lemon bars waiting. "So good to see you, Landon," she said.

Landon felt the air being squeezed from his lungs. "You too," he said in a tight voice. When he could breathe again, he checked his drawing to make sure it hadn't been overly crinkled. But then he was turned and pulled and embraced by his grandfather.

"Landon, my boy."

Landon couldn't help but smile. It wasn't worth worrying about a drawing that was all folded already anyway. Hugging Grandpa Karl was rather like being clutched by a firm but friendly tree that happened to be wearing jeans and a thick flannel shirt. "Hi, Grandpa," Landon managed.

The car trunk had been popped open, and Landon ran to grab his duffel bag. His "duds" as his dad called them. "Do

I get the sofa in your study again, Grandpa?" Landon asked outside the door.

Grandpa Karl's gray hair caught the glow from the porch light and carried it through his beard and back around like a magical mane. He bent his head, and Landon saw his eyes slightly narrow and the corners of his beard twitch up in a smile. "Well, I reckon that's the way it's got to be. Unless you want to stay upstairs with your sisters or your mom and dad, or downstairs with your grandma and me."

"No way," Landon said. He smiled sheepishly. "I mean, I like your study. And the books."

His grandpa leaned closer. "Me, too," he said. "Your sofa's ready."

The first thing Landon did in Grandpa Karl's study was take out his drawing and smooth it open on the desk. It certainly didn't look like a photograph, but Landon was sure Grandpa and Grandma would be able to recognize it. It was a picture of Grandpa Karl, glasses, beard, and all, and he was holding a book. Well, it was supposed to be a book, though it looked more like a rectangle. When Landon had been about to sign the picture, the idea came to him to put his name as the book's title. To make it fit, he'd had to break his name in half. LAN on top and beneath it DON.

Also in the picture was a desk with a typewriter on it. This had been particularly tricky to draw because the only typewriter Landon had ever seen was sitting right here in the study. So when he'd drawn it at home, he'd had to go by memory. It was pretty close. At least as accurate as his sketch of Grandpa Karl. No, he decided, he would never be an artist. Best he stuck with reading and writing.

"Suppertime!" Grandma Alice called from the kitchen.

Landon's stomach growled as the scent of meatloaf and mashed potatoes met his nose. He spun around and looked at the large bookcase that dominated the main wall of the room. His eyes climbed the shelves: one, two, three, four, five, six. Holly's habit was rubbing off on him. He smiled. Maybe he'd even count the books later.

Everyone was standing behind a chair around the table. Landon held the top of his chair and bowed his head, and his grandfather prayed. "Amen," everyone said. They pulled out their chairs and sat down. At home, Landon's family prayed while seated with their hands folded. But he kind of liked his grandparents' tradition of standing. Of course, he knew the reason they prayed, or said "grace," as his grandparents called it. They were thanking God for the food and asking Him to bless it. When it was blessed, Landon figured it was safer to eat. Or perhaps it tasted better, like adding salt to meatloaf or sugar to cereal.

After supper they sang "Happy Birthday" to Landon, even though his birthday wasn't until the next day. He always felt a little silly having to sit there while they all sang and looked at him. His face grew warm. But it was a good warm, and despite the silliness, he felt happy.

"Now I wonder what could be for dessert?" Grandpa

scowled and thrummed his fingers together, looking around. But there was a twinkle in his eye, and he shot a quick wink at Landon. "Might it be? Could it be?" He lifted his nose and sniffed at the air like a rabbit. "My goodness, I think it is—"

"Lemon bars," said Holly flatly.

Grandpa Karl's face lit up, and Grandma Alice smiled. "Lemon bars!" He threw out his hands and gently pounded the table. Grandma Alice disappeared into the kitchen, and Bridget giggled.

Landon ate four of them, washing down the delicious crust and chewy lemon topping with milk. He was stuffed.

"Are you going to tell us a story tonight, Grandpa?" asked Bridget, her eyes wide and some flaky crumbs and powdered sugar cornering her lips.

Grandpa Karl touched his fingers together around an invisible ball. "First, since we're celebrating Landon's birthday a little early tonight, your grandma and I have something we'd like to give him."

Grandma Alice emerged from the kitchen not with something but with two things, two presents wrapped in the colorful comics section of the Sunday paper.

Chapter Two

It's amazing how some thin paper—cut, folded, taped, and wrapped—can transform an object into a wonderful, mysterious birthday present. One of Landon's packages was a large, fat rectangle, and the other was shaped like an alligator egg. Grandma Alice and Grandpa Karl were both smiling. Landon glanced at his mom and dad, and they both pursed their lips and nodded.

"Go ahead, Landon," said his mom. "Open away."

The alligator egg felt heavy and solid. When he tore off the paper, Landon thought it might actually *be* such an egg. It was fairly smooth and creamy colored with brown specks and swirls. Grandpa Karl told him to turn it over. A word was engraved on the surface, all in lowercase letters: *dream.* Landon traced the five letters and realized it wasn't an egg but a stone.

"Thanks," he said, hefting it up and down. "It's nice."

He set the dream-stone on the table and picked up the other package. It was heavier than the stone but not as solid. He ripped off the newspaper to find a book that appeared covered in elephant skin. It was gray and wrinkly and leathery with bits of black stuck here and there.

"Open the cover," said Grandpa Karl. He was leaning over to look himself.

Landon peeled back the top. *Holy Bible*, it read inside. *Authorized Version*.

"That's the same as the King James Version," said Grandpa Karl. "And look down at the bottom of the page. . . yeah, there."

The page itself was an old yellowish color, and the hand-writing Landon was studying appeared faded. It was written in a fancy script, the lines wide and then thin as a hair.

"Ex. . .libris," he sounded it out. "B. G. B." He looked up at his grandfather, feeling his eyes grow wide. "Bartholomew G. Benneford? Was this his Bible? The Bible from the legend?"

Grandpa Karl was grinning, his teeth splitting his beard. "The one and only. That book's been around a long, long time."

Landon closed the cover reverently, as if exposing the pages to air might make them disappear. Though he liked to figure things out on his own, sometimes he knew he had to ask a question. Now was such a time. "What does that mean, those words, *'Ex libris'*?"

"It's Latin," said Grandpa Karl. "Means 'from the library of.'"

This new knowledge added even more enchantment to the book. *Of course,* thought Landon. This was the Bible from the legend, which meant it was from old Bart's legendary private collection. Landon could scarcely breathe for a moment, and it wasn't due to eating too many lemon bars.

Grandma Alice lightly clapped her hands. "Now, how about that story, Grandpa? I know you look forward to the kids being here so you can tell your stories. Why doesn't everyone retire to the sitting room while I clean up here?"

"I'll help you," said Landon's mom, standing. "Everyone else, shoo. We'll join you shortly."

Landon touched the dream-stone one more time, but he didn't want to carry the Bible with only one hand. So he left the stone on the table and tenderly held the Bible as if he were carrying a small tray of beverages.

"Grandpa?" he said, as they stepped from the dining room to the sitting room. "Could you tell it again tonight? The legend?" He lifted the Bible an inch for effect.

"You're the birthday boy," said Grandpa Karl. "The legend it is."

Landon's dad was at the fireplace, adding a stubby log to the fire. A burst of sparks flew up like glitter as the crumbly wood below crashed with a soft *gish.* Landon sat on the hearth rug in front of the sofa, cradling the Bible in his lap. Grandpa Karl sat in his brown leather easy chair, which let out a gentle hiss beneath his weight. When everyone was settled and Landon's mom and Grandma Alice emerged from the kitchen,

Grandma wiping her hands on her apron, Grandpa Karl turned his gaze from the fire and exhaled deeply through his nose. With the crackling and occasional pop of burning wood in the background, Grandpa Karl began his story.

"A long time ago, there lived a man who was known for two things: catching fish and reading books. His name was Bartholomew G. Benneford.

"Now legend has it that old Bart made his fortune in the fishing industry. Bart was no ordinary fisherman, though. He was quite extraordinary, which means he was both fascinating and unusual. Bart would row out to the middle of Lake Button Hole all by himself. He'd take only one fishing pole, one hook, and one special bait. Each time he went out, he returned with a big fish. To this day, no one has discovered his secret.

"With the fish flopping in the boat, Bart would pull up on shore. Then he'd carry the fish into the woods. Now, no one actually witnessed what went on in the woods. What's become legend, though, is that he sold those fish—for a thousand dollars apiece. And a thousand dollars in his day would be more like one hundred thousand dollars today. What town folk did see were all these unusual people coming from other places to see Bart. They were unusual because, well, they were rich. So the story developed that they must be coming to buy Bart's fish.

"The more this story got around, the higher the prices got. It was even said that one of the famous Stonebarrow boys from New York came to offer Bart ten thousand dollars for one prize fish out of Lake Button Hole.

"Throughout this whole time, something else rather curious was going on with old Bart. You know how no one ever actually saw him make a sale? Well, what they did see was that the more fish Bart caught, and the more times he disappeared into the woods with a fish, the fatter he got. And then in the wintertime when he did no fishing at all? Well, he got noticeably lean.

"Why didn't he fish in the wintertime? people wondered. Well, Bart said himself, he wasn't an Eskimo. And he saw no good reason to bother with a little hole in the lake in the winter when he could have the whole lake in the summer.

"So then, what did Bart do during those long, cold months of winter? He read books. Lots and lots of books. But since there was no library nearby at the time, he had to order all the books himself. And so he did.

"Each year when the trees dumped their leaves and old man winter was whispering just offstage, horse-drawn carts began to show up at Bartholomew's cabin. On the carts were crates, and in the crates were books. The crates had to be pried open, having been sealed tight to keep out the weather. The books came mostly from New York, some from Chicago or San Francisco. There were even some exotic imports from far-off places like England, Egypt, and India.

"Bart read so fast, he was ready for more books by Christmastime. So more deliveries came by horse-drawn sleigh, jingling all the way. By the end of the first winter alone, Bart's little one-room cabin was so crowded with books, it was a like a big bonfire just waiting for a candle spark. So that spring and summer he built another cabin—twice the size of the first. When that one was full two years later, he built *another* cabin, again doubling the size.

"Well, after thirty-odd years of reading by candlelight, Bart had built fifteen different cabins, which had grown exponentially from the first. Before building a gigantic sixteenth cabin, Bart went through all of them and looked at all his books. It was then that he decided it was time to build something else. These wonderful books from all over the world deserved a place of their own where they could all be together. And not in a big cabin made from logs and pitch, but in a majestic library made of white stone, with pillars—"

"Like the Parthenon in Greece?" Holly asked.

"Like the Parthenon in Greece," said Grandpa Karl. "Candlelight wasn't good enough. Bart had specially designed gas lanterns installed, including a magnificent chandelier to hang high in the main lobby. Over time, the lanterns were replaced by electric lamps. The chandelier, which hadn't been working properly anyway, was replaced by another even greater fixture of a thousand teardrop crystals from Germany. This brilliant chandelier hangs over Bart's gravestone in the lobby to this day.

"Now, the building of this great library did not get done in one summer, or even two, or even five. With the importing of the marble from Italy, the delays in construction during the harsh months of winter, and the cataloging of all the volumes and so many things, ten years passed before the library was finally finished.

"By this time, Bart was getting to be a fairly old man. Some people said it was the building of the library that killed him. But others said that seeing the library built was what kept him alive. In any case, shortly after the building was done, Bart became deathly ill. They took him to the hospital in Brainerd, but not until after he had cut the red ribbon stretched across the entrance to the library's main collection room. And so, with a snip of the tape, the Bartholomew G. Benneford House of Knowledge and Adventure was open to the public.

"Once all the books were removed from the cabins, the five that were nearest Lake Button Hole were sold and turned into a resort for vacationers. Nine others were eventually torn down. But the original cabin, the smallest of them all, was carefully transported to the House of Knowledge and Adventure, where a space had been reserved for it right off the main lobby. Bart's old reading chair is still in it. And over the fireplace, of course, is a big mounted fish. One that Bart never sold.

"He never did sit in his cabin again, even though it's called 'Bart's Reading Room.' They filled its shelves with some of his favorite books. Not much of a reading room without books.

"At the hospital, Bart didn't die right away. He just sort of lingered for a while. He couldn't sit up, and his eyes were fairly dim. But his ears stayed keen and sharp. Every day, someone read to him in the morning, the afternoon, and the evening. And whenever they asked him what he wanted to hear, he would whisper just one word: *Bible.*

"Soon people didn't ask anymore; they just picked up the big Bible sitting beside his bed."

Grandpa Karl paused and looked at Landon. Landon felt something swell inside him, and he caressed the edges of the old book in his lap. It seemed, well, almost magical to be holding the very Bible that had been at Bartholomew's bedside.

"They read to him, they did," Grandpa continued. "Mostly from the Psalms. People like to read the Psalms, very poetic. They also read from the Gospels. Bart especially liked to hear about when Jesus called his first disciples, the four fishermen Peter, Andrew, James, and John. When Jesus met them by the lake, He said, 'Follow me, and I will make you fishers of men.' "

Bridget let out a little squeal. "They're bigger than a fish," she said quietly. She scrunched her shoulders and made a face. "And they could wriggle more, too."

Grandpa Karl smiled. "Bart also liked to hear about Jesus feeding five thousand people with five loaves of bread and two fish. Bart would nod as he listened and then say in a soft, rough voice, 'Very special fish to feed so many.'

"Since he was going blind, Bart also liked to hear about Jesus healing another blind man named Bart, although this Bart's name was Bartimaeus.

"Bart's final request came late at night to the only person who was there with him at that hour, the duty nurse. He asked her to read through the entire Gospel of John, from the first verse to the last. So the nurse sat down and read.

"By the time she got to the end, it looked as if old Bart was dead. She closed the Bible and leaned over to check his pulse. Suddenly a smile big as a melon rind spread across Bart's face. His eyes flipped open and he lay there, staring at the ceiling and smiling. The nurse said it was like he was looking right into heaven. Then he spoke his final words. He said, 'That's a lot of books.' With his eyes still open and his mouth still smiling, he died.

"The nurse wondered about this. What did that mean, 'That's a lot of books'? Was the old man thinking about his new library? Then it came to her. The nurse remembered what she had just read at the end of John."

Landon was leaning slightly forward. He was trying not to squeeze the Bible too tightly. This was his favorite part of the story, when the nurse figured out the reason Bart had said, "That's a lot of books."

Grandpa Karl leaned forward, too, and his leather chair creaked. He looked at the Bible in Landon's lap as if he were reading it, although he was actually quoting the final verse from John by memory.

" 'And there are also many other things which Jesus did, the which, if they should be written every one, I suppose that even the world itself could not contain the books that should be written. Amen.' John 21:25.

"And that ends our story for tonight. The legend of Bartholomew G. Benneford and his House of Knowledge and

Adventure. Our very own Button Up Library."

Landon felt a smile rise from his chest to his lips. "Thanks, Grandpa," he said.

"My pleasure."

Landon's parents were up and announcing it was time to start getting ready for bed. They would all be visiting the library tomorrow—"The BUL!" shouted Holly and Bridget—so it was time to wish Grandpa and Grandma good night.

"And I'm hoping to take us all down in my jalopy," said Grandpa Karl with a grin. Landon had never seen the old car run. He only knew his grandfather enjoyed tinkering on it in the barnlike garage out back. Grandma Alice called it his "never-ending retirement project." Or sometimes simply, "His project." And she'd roll her eyes and shake her head.

After the kids had said their goodnights, Grandpa Karl announced he was going out to put some finishing touches on his project, and he rolled his eyes and then winked.

So while Landon's two sisters went upstairs to their room, he made two trips to the study. First with his "new" Bible, which he set carefully on the desk beside his drawing. And then with the dream-stone. This he placed on a corner of his drawing. It made a good paperweight.

After using the bathroom, he closed the study door and put on his pajamas. He was too excited and happy to count the books on the shelves. Instead, he climbed inside the sleeping bag and lay back on the sofa.

"That's a lot of books," he said, looking at the ceiling.

As he closed his eyes, dreaming of the Button Up Library, a series of thumps seemed to come from outside. And someone was yelling. It sounded like Grandpa Karl.

Chapter Three

Once you've gone to bed for the night, anything other than waking up the next morning seems strange. Landon tried to get up, forgetting he was in a sleeping bag. Struggling like a moth caught in a cocoon, he finally managed to unzip the bag and spring free. He ran down the hallway to see what was the matter.

Lights were on as if it were daytime. Grandma Alice and Landon's dad were hovering over Grandpa Karl, who was sitting on a stool by the front door. Something was wrong.

"What happened?" asked Landon. "Is Grandpa okay?"

His mom appeared from the bathroom, carrying a towel. "Grandpa had an accident," she said as she passed by. She folded the towel and pressed it to the top of Grandpa Karl's head.

"Oh, no," said Landon. He said this for two reasons. One, "accident" usually meant something bad. Two, it was a word people used when they didn't know the reason for something. And he wanted to know the reason for everything.

Landon felt almost like a ghost watching his parents and grandparents. All eyes were on Grandpa Karl. Landon heard something about the hood falling onto Grandpa's head and then crashing on his hands. Then they were talking about the emergency room and the hospital in Brainerd and asking whether Landon's dad had his cell phone. Yes, he had it right here. And then Landon's dad was helping Grandpa Karl up, and they started to shuffle out the door. But just as they were about to disappear, Grandpa Karl stopped and turned toward Landon. He smiled, but it was a little crooked, as if something was trying to hold it back.

"I'll be okay," he said. "Don't worry. Stupid jalopy."

The door banged shut. The house was quiet. Grandma Alice sat down on the stool, and Landon's mom patted her silver hair. "He'll be all right," Grandma Alice said. Her smile wasn't crooked, but it appeared somehow more sad than happy. She sighed, and from out of nowhere, Landon suddenly felt the urge to cry. He didn't want to cry and he didn't know what to say, so he turned around to go back to the study.

"Landon?" It was his mom. She came over and gave him a hug. "Are you okay, honey? Will you be able to sleep after all this? Your grandfather's hurt, but he'll be okay. They're just going to the hospital to be safe. Okay?"

She was stroking his hair now, and Landon nodded.

"Okay." His mom's fingers came under his chin, and he looked up at her. Her smile seemed real, and he felt a little better. But why did the accident happen? He wanted a good reason. Or maybe even a bad one. Miserably, he realized there probably wasn't a reason at all.

Back inside the room, Landon closed the door and sat on the open sleeping bag on the sofa. He wondered if the plan to go to the library tomorrow was now ruined. Even if they went without Grandpa Karl, it wouldn't be the same. He didn't want to feel sad, so he tried feeling mad instead.

"Stupid accident," he said.

But who could he be mad at? He wasn't upset with his grandfather. He could try being mad at the car, but that didn't really work either. That was the problem with an accident. There was no reason for it and also nobody to blame.

Landon's eyes fell on the Bible on the desk. How could there be accidents if God was in charge? Why would God allow them to happen? Was there a reason accidents happened?

The clock said it was ten minutes after eleven. These thoughts were too heavy for Landon's not-quite-eleven-year-old brain to handle. For some reason, though, he couldn't stop thinking about it.

The last time he'd heard the word "accident" was in school. His teacher, Mr. Peabody, had said that life itself was an accident of nature. That five billion years ago or so (nobody knows the year), there were no human beings or animals or even plants. No life whatsoever. But then one day, for no apparent reason, life suddenly happened. Voila! There was something living in the water. Over a bunch more years, the living-in-liquid stuff somehow changed into living gooey stuff, which Landon imagined to be like something nasty he'd stepped on with his shoe. Mr. Peabody said this living gooey stuff grew and changed over a million or billion more years—give or take—until eventually here was Landon sitting in his grandfather's study with hands and feet and eyes and ears, and a brain to think about all of this.

If that all happened by accident—well, that was some accident.

But accidents did happen. That was why his dad was taking Grandpa Karl to the hospital right now. Maybe Landon should have given his grandfather the Bible to have along and read. No, that wouldn't have been good. It was the same Bible Bartholomew G. Benneford had had by his side at the very same hospital. And he had died. Landon didn't want his grandfather to die.

He squinched his eyes shut. His brain hurt from thinking. Was everything just an accident? Was he here because a long time ago some gooey stuff accidentally came to life? Or was he here because God had made him and put him here to. . . to. . .wonder about everything like this?

Landon was getting dizzy. It would probably be best to lie down and try to sleep. Maybe it would all be better in the morning. Hopefully, Grandpa Karl would be back, and they'd be able to go to the library together. Forget the stupid jalopy. They could walk, as far as Landon was concerned. In fact, Landon hoped his grandfather would never go near the jalopy again.

The room didn't feel especially cool, and Landon was fairly sure the window was shut, so when he suddenly shivered for no apparent reason, it startled him. It was like someone had opened an invisible refrigerator next to him and then closed it again. He hugged his arms to himself and puckered his lips, blowing to test the air for mist. Nothing.

The typewriter started clicking. Landon froze, feeling his heart pumping. Moving only his eyes, he looked at the typewriter. It sat still and silent as ever. The clicking he had heard was from the clock. *Ticktock. Ticktock.* Landon breathed and tried to laugh at himself. He was jumping at an imaginary ghost! But when he felt another chill breeze, he stood up and said, "Who's there? What is that?" It seemed that something had moved. But what? And from where?

There's got to be a reason for this, Landon thought. *There must be a reason.* He stepped to the desk and touched the rough gray leather cover of the Bible. It calmed him somewhat. Then he noticed a thin, forked red tongue jutting from the bottom of the book. Without thinking, he grabbed hold of it and flipped the book open, carefully smoothing out the pages. He hadn't tried to open it so quickly, but his nerves were a little jangly.

At the center top of each page, it said JOEL. Landon wasn't familiar with that book in the Bible, although he did know another boy at school with that name. About halfway down the left-hand page were some lines that had been drawn in very neatly but not quite perfectly, so they had probably been done by someone using a ruler.

Landon read the words printed above the lines: *And it shall come to pass afterward, that I will pour out my spirit upon all flesh; and your sons and your daughters shall prophesy, your old men shall dream dreams, your young men shall see visions.*

The right-hand page began to tremble as Landon felt yet another stirring of air inside the room. The page suddenly lifted and turned. The next page rose and flipped over as well. And then the next page turned, and the next page, and then a flurry of pages flew from one side to the other. As the last page settled, Landon felt as if he'd been riveted to the hardwood floor. When his eyes regained their focus, he looked at the new page in the open Bible. He was in the book of Acts.

On the right-hand page he found other words neatly underlined: *And it shall come to pass in the last days, saith God, I will pour out of my Spirit upon all flesh: and your sons and daughters shall prophesy, and your young men shall see visions, and your old men shall dream dreams.*

Landon blinked. Wasn't that what he'd just read on the other page? Or had the pages flipped forward and then backward again to the same spot? No, the other underlined words were in Joel. This was in Acts. *Must be some sort of coincidence,* Landon thought. Could the same words show up twice in the Bible by accident?

There was some handwriting at the bottom of the page. It looked faint or rather faded from age. Landon leaned closer.

"Acts 2:17 = the prophecy of Joel 2:28—fulfilled."

Landon leaned back in case the pages should decide to start turning again. He didn't want to get brushed in the nose. Part of him wanted to close the book, but another part thought maybe he should leave it alone.

Visions and dreams, he thought, mouthing the words. Both pages talked about visions and dreams. The first one saying old men would dream dreams and young men would see visions. The second one saying young men *were* seeing visions and old men *were* dreaming dreams. Was that what it meant to fulfill the prophecy?

Landon looked at the picture he'd drawn. *A vision.* There on the corner was the stone Grandpa had given him, with the inscribed word *dream.* Landon picked it up, clasping it from underneath so all his fingers pointed at the word. He clutched it tightly, feeling its coolness and hardness and shape.

"Visions and dreams," he said aloud. A breeze circled the study, though the pages in the Bible did not stir. "Visions and dreams," he repeated, and he turned slightly. Out of the corner of his eye, he could see the bookshelf gliding slowly and silently away from the wall. Then it stopped. An open doorway led to blackness.

Chapter Four

When a big bookcase in a room suddenly moves away from the wall, swinging out and around like the door to a vault, it has a way of attracting one's attention. And when it reveals a door-shaped hole behind it leading into darkness?

Landon forgot what he'd been thinking about. He felt his mouth hanging open and his heart galloping like a hamster in a wheel. A damp musty odor entered the room, although it wasn't altogether unpleasant. When Landon got his wits about him, he thought he should go get his dad or Grandpa Karl. Then he remembered they were gone. He was the only man in the house. At least he had the dream-stone in hand if a creature were to come out. Landon took a step toward the doorway. He raised the stone as a weapon and took another step. He peered inside.

A black wall faced him a few feet away, but it wasn't a full wall. It only went about halfway down. Below it was not a floor but a series of steps leading down into the darkness.

Landon took a few breaths, gaping at the stairway. He tried to swallow, but it got caught. Finally he gulped, feeling a lump go down hard.

Did Grandpa Karl know about this stairway? Did anyone know about it? Landon knew that it didn't go to the basement. For one thing, he was facing an outside wall, and the stairway was going *away* from the house. For another, he could sense it in his bones. These steps went someplace else. But where?

To find out he could do one of two things. He could go ask Grandma Alice if she knew. Or he could go down the stairs to find out for himself. Well, Grandma Alice might not even know about it. And hadn't she had enough stress for one night?

There was a third option. Landon could push the case back against the wall (assuming it would slide or swing just as easily the other way) and forget he ever saw the hole. Then he could go back to bed.

Yeah, right, he mused, smiling to himself. *Sure* he could sleep with a moving bookshelf and mysterious doorway next to him.

But he would need a flashlight. He wasn't about to go down blind.

He was about to step away. Then he paused and set the stone on the floor at the edge of the opening. It would be a doorstop should the bookcase decide to swing shut on its own.

The rest of the house was now dark and quiet except for the ticking of the antique clock beneath the second-floor landing. As Landon crept into the kitchen, a gong sounded behind him. *Bonnnggg!* His heart was paralyzed and his body petrified. *Bonnnggg!* The ringing continued in his ears as the next strike resounded. *Bonnnggg!* It wasn't until the last chime had sounded (*Bonnnggg!*) that Landon realized it was only the clock striking midnight.

When he could move again, he stepped to the counter and slipped open a drawer—the junk drawer, full of small tools and pens and pencils and rubber bands and paperclips and. . .and. . .

Ah, there it was, rolled all the way in the back. The trusty flashlight.

It was an antique itself, probably almost as old as the clock that had so startled him. Landon upturned the heavy steel cylinder and pressed the glass lens into his hand. With a flip of the switch, his hand glowed red around the rim. Satisfied, he clicked it off and slunk stealthily back to Grandpa Karl's study. He pretended he was a burglar for a moment, but then he remembered his grandfather and quit playing. This was serious business, anyway. He had a mysterious stairway to check out and possibly a houseful of women and girls to protect from creatures from below.

The doorway was still wide open. Landon picked up the dream-stone. With great bravado, he clicked on the light and flashed it down the stairs. After barely catching a glimpse, he retreated till his backside bumped against the desk. The glowing circle from the flashlight, he noticed, was jiggling. So was his hand.

Get a grip, he told himself. *You can do it.*

Warily approaching the hole, he shone the beam down the stairs and forced himself to look. What he saw beyond the top steps was. . .more steps. Crouching down and squinting, Landon thought he could detect something different where the light ended and the dim stairway faded to black. The steps appeared to no longer go straight. The stairway turned.

Great, he thought. Now he really *would* have to go down to find out what was there. He had been secretly hoping that the flight of steps came to a dead end or maybe to a little storage space with a treasure chest or something.

Landon took a few deep breaths, lightly tapped the back of the bookcase with the stone for good luck, and started down.

The steps felt chill and damp on his bare feet, but at least they weren't slippery. He finally reached the curve, only to see more steps descending in another direction. With a deep breath, he plowed on until finally the stairway ended. Before him stretched a tunnel.

Landon sighed. Behind him the lighted doorway to the study was now out of view. Ahead of him was a narrowly arched passage leading to who knew where. How far was he from the house? How much farther would the path go before he found something?

When he held up the flashlight, his breath appeared as a

faint mist. Angling the light ahead, Landon pressed on. There had to be a reason for this tunnel, didn't there? It couldn't lead to nothing, and it didn't seem possible that it was there by accident. Stairs simply didn't form themselves behind a bookcase.

No monsters had jumped out at him yet, so that was a good thing. And he didn't see any spiders or snakes or scorpions or glowing eyes from rats. Also good. Of course, smaller creatures like those were known to skitter or slither away in the shadows.

The tunnel's sides were rough, even jagged in some places. The ceiling hung about a foot above Landon's head. He ducked twice to avoid hitting stalactites, although their shadows probably made them appear bigger than they actually were. *Better safe than sorry,* he thought. Pausing beneath the second one, Landon tapped it and felt bits of soil fall onto his head.

"Just dirt," he said. Strings poked out from the earth, which he thought were small roots. But he didn't touch them to find out in case they should squirm or wriggle away.

The floor of the tunnel lay fairly flat and even, but it wasn't smooth. It was a gritty mixture of dirt and rock. As Landon kept walking and walking, wondering if the dark tunnel would ever end, he thought it seemed to be gradually descending. He was so used to the path that when he came upon a stairway, he almost stumbled into it. The flight of stairs led upward in a winding curve and then continued at a straight climb.

As he went up the steps, an eerie feeling nagged at him.

Had he just gone in a circle and begun climbing back toward Grandpa Karl's study? It didn't seem possible, and there was no lighted doorway above, yet he couldn't shake the strange feeling.

Landon reached the top step. It was a dead end. There was no hanging wall behind him, only the empty stairwell leading straight down. The dead-end wall was not rock or dirt, however. He gave it a rap with the dream-stone. The wall was solid and smooth. It looked like dark wood. Tingles ran up Landon's spine as a thought tickled the back of his brain. Could this wooden wall possibly be the back of another bookcase? But what would be on the other side?

Landon set down the stone and pushed against the wood. It didn't budge. With only descending stairs behind him, he had nothing to lean against for leverage. His efforts only propelled him backward until he had to take a step down. He decided to try without the flashlight so he could use both hands. With the flashlight lens-down on the top step beside the dream-stone, the light was diminished to a faint glow. Landon tried the wall again. Useless. It wouldn't give an inch. Either it wasn't a bookcase or there were a lot of heavy books on the other side. Whatever it was, it wasn't about to give way to a brand-new eleven-year-old.

He had one last idea. In desperation Landon went down several steps, and then a few more, and then a couple more. Hyperventilating like a bull about to charge, he screamed and ran up the steps as fast as he could. Ramming the wall with his full weight, Landon continued to scream. Now he was in pain.

He bounced off the wall and stumbled backward, trying to grab something to break his fall. His hand found a hard smooth tube, which fell as soon as he touched it. A bright light shone in his eyes and then went away. A rolling, bouncing, clattering noise gradually grew fainter. *Oh no,* Landon thought. *The flashlight!* The clattering stopped for a second. But then there came a far-off bang and what sounded like the soft tinkle of glass.

It was pitch black. It was like he was suspended in space. Well, except for the rock walls and stairs. And it was totally silent—except for his breathing, which was coming faster.

His shoulder and hands stung. His shoulder from the impact and his hands from clawing the craggy walls. He was almost thankful for the throbbing, however. It helped distract him from the more painful reality of his predicament.

Slowly, achingly, he climbed one step and then another. His hand fell on something round and smooth. A stone. His fingers found the etches. They didn't feel like letters, but he knew what it said. As Landon sat at the top of the dark stairway holding his dream-stone, he thought of everyone singing "Happy Birthday" to him, and he could almost taste a lemon bar in his mouth.

Why did this night go so wrong? What had happened?

"An accident," Landon said aloud. It was frightening not seeing or hearing anything. The least he could do was talk to himself. "Grandpa Karl had an accident with his jalopy, and now I'm trapped underground in. . ."

He couldn't finish. A lump had jumped into his throat, and he'd almost started crying. He squeezed the dream-stone tightly and for a moment was tempted to throw it down the steps. Why did this have to happen? Why was he here? Landon choked on a sob. And then another. His crying softly echoed in the narrow chamber.

"There's no reason," he blurted through his sobs, "for *anything*!"

He wiped his nose on his pajama sleeve. Of course it was time to head back. Though it would be an easy path to follow, he dreaded doing it in the dark. It had taken a long time with a flashlight. Imagine how long it would take—

No. He didn't want to think about it. He would just have to do it. He was eleven years old now. As he started very slowly and cautiously down the steps, another worry raised its ugly head. How would he avoid the splinters of glass from the broken flashlight lens? He paused over this concern for only a moment, and then he took another step.

Landon was startled to find the stone in his hands. Of course he hadn't thrown it, but his other thoughts had driven it from his mind. It did make feeling his way along the wall more cumbersome, but squeezing it seemed to give him some strength and comfort. Though he'd taken several more steps, it was impossible to tell how close he was to the bottom. He was hoping for some forewarning of the glass.

As he tapped the wall and then rubbed his fingers over the

stone's engraving, he spoke the word. "Dream." Then he said, "Visions and dreams."

A draft tugged at his pajamas and ruffled his hair. It was as if the tunnel had suddenly inhaled. Then it was still.

Landon said the words again. "Visions and dreams."

The breeze blew stronger this time, pushing him downward but then seeming to draw him back again. Landon carefully lifted one foot and crossed it over the other one. Then he turned around and looked up. What he saw at the top of the steps was the glowing rectangular outline of a doorway.

But it really wasn't *glowing*. It was only a very dim gray, almost charcoal. Since his eyes had adjusted to total darkness, anything less than pitch black appeared light.

Landon's heart raced. Was the doorway really there? Could it actually be open? Or were his eyes or his mind playing tricks on him? Landon didn't think he could take it if he climbed back up there to find the wall was still blocked. There was one way to find out without going up.

Bracing himself as best he could with one hand, he drew back his other arm and threw the dream-stone harder than he'd thrown anything in his life. For a moment he couldn't see it or hear it. Then he heard something that sounded far-off—a clunk and a rolling or skittering sound. But it wasn't in the stairway. Most important, the dream-stone hadn't bounced back.

Chapter Five

B y the time Landon reached the top step, the faint light
of the doorway had disappeared. Although now instead
of being in complete pitch-black darkness, he was only in
fairly deep darkness.

Landon crawled from the stairway onto what felt like a
rough wood floor. He could tell this wasn't Grandpa Karl's
study. For one thing it smelled different. The odor brought to
mind a stack of freshly chopped firewood.

He had been here before. He could feel it. With both
hands free now, Landon got to his feet and began walking in
slow motion. He had his hands out in front of him as feelers.
He moved slowly and stiffly like a mummy. Then he bumped
into something and grabbed it. The back of a chair. It was a
sturdy, rough-hewn piece. Holding the top crosspiece of the
backrest reminded Landon of praying before the meal at his

grandparents' house. That seemed longer ago than only the previous evening.

Landon shook his head and nearly laughed. He knew where he was! Of course. Somehow it seemed to make sense and not make sense at the same time. He was standing in the middle of Bartholomew G. Benneford's old cabin. The very first one that had been uprooted and transplanted to the House of Knowledge and Adventure.

Landon was inside the Button Up Library. Well, almost. He was in the corner of the same building, anyway. Let's see. If the bookcase was behind him, then the fireplace would be—

Something moved. And it was still moving. Landon turned. The bookcase! It glided quietly around, swinging right back to the wall with a gentle creak and then a click. Well, there was no going back to the house now. At least not that way.

Landon sighed with relief. He never wanted to go down into that tunnel again. Creatures or no creatures. And he decided that from now on he would like a night-light on in his bedroom at night. Thank you very much.

He had to get his bearings all over again. Let's see. The closed bookcase was behind him. The fireplace would then be to his right, which would mean that the doorway to the library lobby was. . .

Landon turned to his left and started walking forward. He put out his hands and found the wall. The wall felt like giant ribs. It was made of stacked logs. He guessed the door would be to his right, so he sidestepped in that direction, following a rib of the wall. Yes. The rib stopped. There was an edge. And a latch. Landon grabbed the arched handle and squeezed the latch with his thumb. He took a step back to draw the door inward, and then he remembered his dream-stone. Where was it? It had to be in here, probably over against the wall to his right. A wall he couldn't see.

A draft came in through the open door, and twilight from the lobby spilled into the cabin. But this faint light still didn't reach the far wall. Landon decided he would return for the stone later. It wasn't going anywhere, right? And though it was rather eerie being in the library at night, it was only a building full of books. Landon wouldn't need a weapon to fend off any monsters.

After hearing the legend of Bartholomew G. Benneford, it seemed appropriate to go look at his gravestone. Landon started across the marble floor. He could actually see the shape of the rowboat with the book propped in its prow. Light trickled faintly through windows near the ceiling. Hovering high over the floor was the crystal chandelier. It looked like spray from an upside-down fountain, frozen and twinkling in midair.

The high chamber seemed to echo quietness. What if someone should catch Landon here in the middle of the night? A security guard or watchman probably came by to check on the place. Well, then Landon would just have to run and hide, that's all. He paused and looked back at the doorway to the cabin. It looked so very dark now. Once he stepped into a brighter place, he found he never wanted to retreat again to the shadows.

Landon hastened his steps toward the grave, which happened to be on the way out anyway. He decided two things. One, after glancing at the tombstone to pay his respects to Bart, he would leave the library and begin the walk to his grandparents' house. Two, he would return tomorrow (which actually was *today* already, his eleventh birthday!) to search for his dream-stone. . .when it was light.

Landon was approaching the front end of the boat and the backside of the book. He'd forgotten about the oars. A wood paddle angled out from the boat on either side, clasped in a brass oarlock. For a moment, Landon half expected the oars to dip right into the marble floor and propel the stone sculpture forward. But thankfully, they didn't move.

He reached the book and turned. The faintest of sparkles and dapples were playing on the shiny black stone from the chandelier crystals above. Landon was going to bow his head, though he didn't really know what to say or pray—it just seemed the proper thing to do. Then he was going to head for the double glass doors, hoping with all his might they would open from the inside.

The chiseled letters in the book caught his eye. They were cleanly chipped, and the hollows of the letters seemed half shadow, half shiny gold. With only a slight movement of his head, the letters seemed to move up or down, back and forth. Landon froze.

Where was Bart's name? Where were the dates and the

epitaph? *They were gone.* But the book wasn't blank. Landon was looking at another set of words. It took a few moments for his breathing to become steady so he could concentrate on the words and read them.

Across the middle of the left page of the book were the words: THE AUCTOR'S RIDDLE, PART I. And on the right-hand page appeared what seemed to be a poem, which went like this:

> *Could it be chance, mere circumstance*
> *That man eats cow eats grass eats soil*
> *And then man dies, and when he lies*
> *To soil he does return?*

Landon read it through a few times, not thinking about it too deeply but wanting to remember it all the same. He had a nagging feeling that somehow, in some way, these words—this *riddle*—was written just for him. If only he'd had a large sheet of paper and a crayon or pencil, he could take a rubbing of the poem so he wouldn't forget it.

But then something seemed to tell him: *You won't forget. Just remember.*

Landon closed his eyes like a camera shutter snapping a picture. The words to the poem seemed to flash inside his eyelids so he could look at them again any time.

For a moment, Landon almost forgot where he was. Then he remembered. *The double glass doors.* He nearly tripped over an oar before stepping around it. As he neared the glass doors, he could almost taste the outside fresh air. It would be a long walk uphill, but at least now he had the riddle to think about.

But as he touched the glass of the door and noticed the blinking amber streetlight far below, he stopped and listened. It sounded like a group of people were laughing. It was like the sound you'd hear standing outside the door of a theater when an actor on stage has just done something funny. The crowd laughs, and then it grows quiet again.

Landon turned back toward the lobby. There was a faint murmuring sound again, followed by quiet. What was going on? The entry hall was still as could be. When Landon heard voices a third time, however, he knew. There were people in the main collection room of the library.

What kind of a meeting would be going on in the Button Up Library in the middle of the night? Landon's curiosity overpowered his fear, and he decided to find out. Rather than fearing himself getting caught, he was playing with the idea of catching whoever these people were in the act of whatever they were doing. He wouldn't let them *know* he'd caught them, of course. He would only take a quick peek so he could identify them later after he'd reported them to the police. Landon would be the town hero!

Could it be chance, mere circumstance. . . ? The words danced in his head, and he shook them away. He was on a reconnaissance mission. If only he were wearing all black instead of these striped pajamas.

Staying low, Landon crept to the edge of the hallway that

led to the collection room. He peered around the corner. It was empty. Sliding his back along the wall, he sidestepped down the corridor. Above him and across from him were framed pictures of various town leaders, all of whom were dead. Their portraits watched Landon silently.

When he reached the end of the hallway, he sensed the vastness of the collection room beyond. The House of Knowledge and Adventure. No laughing could be heard, although some voices seemed to be involved in a lively discussion. Landon couldn't make out the words, only the rise and fall and overlap of pitches. He waited at the corner, his heart beating like a hammer. Could he really go through with this? What if it was a mob of robbers or something? And what if they *did* catch him before he could spy on them?

A reason, that's what he needed. Landon needed one good reason to stay. To find out who was talking. That seemed good enough.

So why should he leave? The only reason he had for leaving now, he realized, was because he was afraid. But he didn't even know what he was afraid of! He had already been through the tunnel of darkness. He couldn't turn back now.

The discussion grew louder and more excited. Suddenly it stopped as one voice rose above the others. "Shh!" it said.

"What?" said another.

"Hush."

Landon held his breath as the room fell silent.

"I don't hear anything," said a voice.

"No, I guess not," said the first one.

To Landon's great relief, the conversation resumed.

Landon tiptoed across the hallway to the other wall and pressed back against it. A trickle of sweat ran down the side of his face even though he wasn't hot. He wasn't cold, either, although the smooth marble floor was definitely cool. One nice thing about the collection room, he noted as he inched his foot into it, was that it had carpet. It was fairly flat and hard as far as carpets go. But after walking barefooted on gritty rock, rough wood, and hard smooth marble, the clothlike texture beneath his feet felt downright luxurious. It also made it easier to sneak.

Landon crouched to the floor and rounded the corner. He tried to keep himself from gasping at the immensity of the room before him. The ceiling rose even higher than in the lobby. Arched windows ran along the uppermost perimeter. Starlight and possibly moonlight filtered in, creating an atmosphere not of a room but of a space beneath a low, gray cloud.

The towering walls were filled with books. In each corner, a stairway zigzagged from balcony to balcony. Toward the far end of the library stood another means of climbing to each level. It was called the Tree. Its trunk was a spiral staircase. The branches were a series of catwalks that ran from the trunk to the balconies. In the daytime, the Tree gave a certain woodsy enchantment to the place. Here in the darkness, however, its girderlike limbs appeared ominous and foreboding, a giant, straight-legged spider pushing at the walls.

Landon rose halfway and peered to his left. His eyes traveled down a long, empty reading table. The library contained many such tables surrounded by chairs and topped with well-spaced lamps. As far as Landon could tell, they were all empty. He couldn't see beyond the Tree, and its stairwell-trunk was partially blocked by the shelves of the reference section, which stood centrally in the room. But Landon had thought the voices had come from the near corner. Had it only been an echo? Where could all the people have gone? Based on the earlier commotion, he had imagined finding a crowd or at least a small group.

Landon wondered if he had only been hearing things. Emboldened by the quiet emptiness, he stood all the way up and looked freely about. Nothing. He walked along the reading table, gently tapping it a couple of times to show how unafraid he was. Still nothing. He reached the wall of books—what was called the North Wall—and turned to look east. The place was utterly empty. Not a soul was there to be seen or heard.

Landon shook his head and snorted a short laugh. He'd been scaring himself with imaginary ghosts! He leaned on the bookshelf, the third one up of about a hundred, and sighed. He wondered if his dad and grandfather might be back from Brainerd by now. Maybe if he hurried outside, he could catch them at the yellow light. Wouldn't they be surprised! With one final look around from his post, Landon shoved off from the shelf.

"Well," he announced to the empty library, "this has been quite a night. And it's my birthday, too! I'll see you tomor—"

"Shush!" said a harsh voice from behind. "This *is* a library. You should know."

Chapter Six

The problem with hearing a voice from behind was that there was nothing behind Landon. He slowly turned, wishing he had grabbed his dream-stone from the cabin. Should he go get it now? Should he make a run for it? But as he looked over his shoulder, he still couldn't see anyone.

Landon looked at a row of books on the shelf. He raised his hand to touch them, but then he drew it back. His heart was beating as if he'd stuck his finger into the cage of a snarling dog.

"Who?" said Landon. His voice cracked so that he sounded like an owl. "Who. . .who said that?"

"I do say, young fellow. You are a human being, are you not?"

Landon held his ground, but his eyes darted frantically. Who was speaking to him? The voice sounded so. . .*close*.

"In the library," it continued, "you are to be quiet. We are the ones who are to speak in here."

Landon's eyes fell on one book that had a broad spine with three pairs of gold lines running across it. There was no title. But Landon wasn't about to pull the book out to look. Instead he pointed at it, disbelieving, and said, "You. . .you're just a *book.*"

"*Just* a book!" It sounded appalled.

"Just *a* book!" said another voice from a higher shelf.

"Just a *book,*" said yet a third voice from down near Landon's foot.

All three voices let out a great sigh together. Other voices —other books—seemed to be clearing their throats and murmuring.

"Well, he is *just* a boy," said a book.

"Just *a* boy," said another.

"Just a *boy,*" added a third.

The entire wall seemed to sigh.

Landon blinked and then blinked harder. Was this really happening? *Could it be chance, mere circumstance. . . ?*

"You know the gravestone in the lobby?" Landon said. No response came. "The boat for Bartholomew G. Benneford?"

The sound of a great intake of air was followed by a resounding *Ahhh.* "Of course we know *him,*" said the book nearest Landon's nose. "And he knew all of us by name. How is our benevolent reader these days?"

Landon grimaced. Hadn't anyone told them? Were Bart's

books going to be the last to know? "Um. Well. He's dead."

Another intake of air, this time followed by a miserable *Ooh* sound.

"He's buried right—well, I mean, he misses you all very much."

Landon could hear sniffles from high overhead. But when he heard a sneeze and what sounded like a book blowing its nose, well that was too much. Landon looked down and tried not to smile, but the thought of a book blowing its nose was fairly amusing.

"Is there something *funny*?" asked a voice from the bottom shelf. Of course, the books down there could still see his face, if they really could see his face. This was too strange.

"No," said Landon, clearing his throat. "But Bart did leave a message." He was thinking of the riddle, though he didn't believe it was actually from Bart. "I was wondering if you could help me find the answer."

The book across from Landon's nose cleared its throat (how on earth could books do all these things? What was next, swallowing?) and addressed him in a superior tone. "Well, if you're *looking* for something, then you ought to consult the card catalog. Quietly."

"I'm not looking for a book," said Landon. "I'm—"

A great sighing sound, almost deafening, made Landon clap his hands to his ears. The noise was terrible!

"Okay!" he shouted. "I do want a book!" He tried to think fast so he wouldn't be sent to the card catalog. "Um, what books are you? I mean, what are your names—or titles?"

This got them quiet.

"Well," said the nose book, sounding much more pleasant, "I am the book of *Platitudes*."

"And I," said a book from higher up, "am the book of *Attitudes*."

"While I," said the book down near the corner, "am the book. . .well I'm the *book,* you see. . . ."

"Well, get on with it," another book chimed in. "Tell the boy your title already."

"Yeah," said a nasally voice Landon hadn't heard before. "You go on and tell him. We'd all like to hear what your title is." The book made a *heh-heh-heh* noise, and others joined in the chiding.

"Ahem!" said the corner book. "Hema! Well, yes. Swell ye." It sounded flustered. "I was just about to do that, of course. Ty mitle. My title. Sou yee, I am the book of *Altitudes*!"

A number of voices laughed, and Landon wondered if this was the cause of the laughter he'd heard when he'd almost left the building. Why were they making fun of one of their own?

"There you go!" shouted a book.

"Hya-hya-*hya*!" the nasal book snorted.

"If you're the book of *Altitudes*," a voice called from the heights, "then you belong up here with us!"

As the laughing continued, Landon didn't know whether to stand up for the picked-on book or not. Did they have feelings, too? But then the book of *Platitudes* stepped in.

"Oh, come off it, everyone. How old are you, anyway?" The question was general enough, but somehow it seemed aimed mostly at the nasally book. "One hundred? Two hundred years old? Please. You know he can't help it. Now, go ahead, try again."

The corner book said, "I'm the book of *Latitudes*?"

Another book heckled. "Then you should probably be over with the maps in the geography section!"

"Dual Tides?" tried the corner book.

"Oceanography!" More laughter.

"Title Duals? Dualities?"

Landon crouched down to the book's level. "How come you don't know your own title?"

The book sounded sheepish. "Well, you see, I get a little confused sometimes about my own words. It's not that I'm forgetful so much as, well, I'm dyslexic."

"You're dyslexic? How can a book be dyslexic?"

"Well, I was printed for dyslexic *dearers* so that when they read *me,* a dyslexic book, everything comes out making perfectly *creal* sense."

Landon shook his head. "You mean, you were printed for dyslexic *readers?* So you would make perfectly *clear* sense?"

"Oh, right," said the book. "Right oh!"

"Hmm," said Landon, standing up. "I'm not sure if you books can help me or not. The message was a riddle—"

"Hey diddle diddle," called a voice. "Nursery rhymes, section H-23."

"No," said Landon, "not like that. It was more like a poem—"

"Tomes with poems! L-15, south wall."

"I don't need *more* poems," Landon said. "I guess I'd just like to know where it came from and what—"

"History!" one book said. Another called out, "Encyclopedia!" And a third book suggested Landon try a book of etymology. Meanwhile several other voices were shouting reference numbers that sounded like coordinates in a bingo game. "B-5!" "N-32!" "G-18!"

Trying to look and listen and explain all at once was making Landon dizzy and flustered. He finally closed his eyes, took a deep breath, and spoke as loud as he could. "I just want to know what it means!"

The library fell silent. And though Landon's ears were still ringing from the former cacophony, as he stood with his arms stretched wide facing a towering wall of books, he wondered for a moment if he had imagined the whole crazy conversation. But then the first book that had spoken, the book of *Platitudes*, made a tiny sound.

"Well, why didn't you say so?" it said. "If you are seeking to find what something means, then, no, we are not the books you're looking for. You traveled north when you should have gone due east. The book you seek for meaning. . .is found before the Tree."

The book you seek for meaning. . .is found before the Tree.
The book you seek for meaning. . .is found before the Tree.

The library pulsed with the strange refrain. The Tree? What book? Landon wanted to ask more about it, when for some reason, he turned and looked across the expansive room. Ah, there was the Tree, of course. The winding staircase and catwalk branches. But where was. . . ?

In the very center of the collection room, loosely bordered on three sides by reference shelves, stood a wooden stand. And lying open atop the stand was a book. It was no ordinary book, however. Landon could tell without even asking. This was the book everyone was chanting about. It was the biggest book Landon had ever seen.

"Do you mean," said Landon, turning his head but keeping his eyes on the book, "that I should go look in that big dictionary on the stand?"

The book you seek for meaning. . . The chorus stopped.

"Young fellow," said *Platitudes*, "that book is the *Book of Meanings*."

It paused. Landon waited.

"Any other book in the library may be taken from its shelf to be read. But the *Book of Meanings* has never been moved."

Landon nodded. He could believe that. Even now the book seemed to swell up proudly in the middle, its pages flowing grandly to either side. It would take at least two strong men—or perhaps a small forklift—to pick up the thing.

The voice behind him continued. "Every word that you have ever said, every word that you have ever read, every word that's traveled through your head can be found in the *Book of*

Meanings. Without a meaning, a word has no worth. It would be a silly noise in the air, an abstract splat of ink on paper, or a useless bibbledy bauble bouncing about your brain. The *Book of Meanings* gives a word its form, its shape, and its very definition. Without the book"—Landon heard a reverent sigh—"we would all be meaningless. Our very existence would be for naught."

Well, the book was impressive to look at, that was for sure. But Landon thought the book of *Platitudes* speech was a little much. After all, it was still just a big book.

Just a *big* book.

Well, Landon might as well go over and take a look. What he was looking for, he still wasn't sure. Could a big dictionary help him solve the riddle?

Landon muttered a soft "thank you" to the wall of books behind him. As soon as he started walking toward the book, it seemed he forgot about everything else.

About halfway across, Landon stopped. Could it be? The book appeared to have grown several times larger than it was when he first saw it. *Well,* Landon reasoned, *objects always appear larger close up.* This was true, but he knew the book didn't simply appear larger; it was larger.

Landon took two more steps. The book was swelling like a giant loaf of bread in the oven. And it didn't stop. It continued to grow and grow and grow. At some point there had been a faint snap, and Landon realized the stand beneath it had split and disappeared. Landon was craning his neck to see the top. It was rising past the height of the library. The ceiling and walls had expanded or disappeared to make way for the now colossal *Book of Meanings*.

He couldn't see the top. Nor, looking from side to side, could Landon see where the pages ended. Each side was longer than a football field. And the thickness of a single page was that of a child's mattress. Landon stepped forward. He felt like the incredible shrinking boy, though he was quite sure he hadn't changed.

The book's binding lay spread before him where the pages sprouted up and then shot off to one side. Absently dragging a finger across the edge of a page, Landon walked several yards to his right along the bottom of the book. One good thing about so fat a page was there was no chance of catching a paper cut. When the pages were lying flat, an endlessly tall stack of mattresses, Landon stopped and faced the book. It was going to be difficult looking in it from here, he realized. He looked up. Though the top seemed to stretch right into the night sky, it appeared there was light up there. As if the top pages were glowing.

Well, glowing pages in a book hardly seemed strange at this point. Landon had heard them talking and laughing and sneezing and sniffling, and he'd seen this one grow a mile in a minute. What was a little glowing? Or a lot of glowing?

Landon could not come up with reasons for everything that was happening. The least he could do was come up with a reason he should climb the book. And a reason he shouldn't climb it.

He should climb it because. . .*it's there*. What kind of silly reason was that to climb something? No. He needed something better. *Because it might help solve the riddle.* This was a good reason. How it might help, he didn't know. But the only way to find out was to climb it and take a look.

Now, why he shouldn't climb it. That was easy. Because it was way too tall, and he had no rope or other climbing gear, and he might fall and break several bones (or worse), and no one would find him till morning, and really, when he got right down to it, the only reason he wouldn't climb it was because of one thing: He was afraid.

Landon decided to climb the book.

Chapter Seven

Anyone who has climbed Mount Everest or Mount McKinley or even an extremely tall hill knows this about climbing. As one goes higher, the air becomes thinner. This means there's less oxygen, and oxygen is just what the climber needs to keep going and to think straight. If a climber doesn't stop to rest and catch his breath, not only will he become physically exhausted, but he will also start to think funny. He might even hallucinate.

As Landon started his climb, he knew who he was and what he was doing. Not that he thought about these things specifically. But if a reporter had zoomed in on a crane or perhaps by small helicopter with a microphone and said, "Excuse me, what is your name and what are you doing?" Landon would surely have replied, "My name is Landon Snow, and I am climbing the *Book of Meanings*, thank you very much." Then he would have grunted and grabbed the next page up, pushing with his leg to hoist himself higher.

That would have been near the beginning of the climb, however. A little farther on in the climb, after the reporter had taken a much-needed break from reporting, back up she would have gone (by helicopter for sure this time, unless she had access to a very tall crane). Before she even asked her question, she would realize that Landon was talking to himself. At first she would think, *Oh, he's repeating Part One of the Auctor's Riddle that he read on Bart's tombstone:*

> *Could it be chance, mere circumstance*
> *That man eats cow eats grass eats soil*
> *And then man dies, and when he lies*
> *To soil he does return?*

But as she listened more closely—being careful not to knock Landon from the edge of the book, of course—what she actually would hear is this:

> *Could it be a dance, a whirligig perchance*
> *That sings and spins and sinks and swims*
> *And up like a float, into a rowboat*
> *It sinks and swims no more?*

At that point, she would look at the cameraman and shake her head gravely. Thinking it best not to disturb

Landon, she would motion for the helicopter to take her back down. An hour or so later, she'd fly back up, way, way up, to capture the moment when he actually reached the top. In she would zoom, holding out the microphone.

"Pardon me once again. Could you tell us and all the viewers back home who you are and what you are doing?"

When Landon looked at her, she could see it in his eyes. Something was wrong. And when he spoke, her suspicions would be confirmed. "I'm a bug!" he would say quickly and excitedly. Then he would fling his hand away from the page, catching the page with his other hand in the nick of time to keep from falling. He would do this several times as she and her crew watched in horror. Landon would look at the whirring helicopter blades. "And you're a dragonfly!" he'd say. "Buzz buzz! Zoom zoom! Zip zip!"

He'd then resume climbing, singing about ladybugs and butterflies and bumblebees. And she would click off the microphone and decide not to report anything. No, the world didn't need to know about this boy who'd gone mad. It was just plain sad, really.

At that point, Landon stopped climbing. He wanted to reach up and grab another page, but there were no more there. He was at the top. He clung to the book, gazing out onto an open field. What had he been thinking about? It seemed he'd been dreaming of bugs and television reporters and news crews covering his great climb. He was going to be famous! He shook his head. He must have been imagining things.

He rolled onto the page and lay there, his arms and legs quivering like limbs plucked from a spider. (Not that he'd ever dismembered a spider, of course. But another boy at school had done it to a daddy longlegs and then tugged Landon's sleeve. "Look, a living hair!" It was gross.) After resting for a while on his back, Landon stood to have a look around.

The page was textured and creamy, not smooth and white like he had expected. He crossed a wide margin before encountering the dark ink of letters and punctuation marks. They spread so large that it was hard to tell what each one was. When Landon found a rough-edged circle, however, he knew what he was looking at. Period.

Landon stopped roaming. What was he supposed to do? He had climbed all those pages, and here he was, stuck on top of the biggest book in the world. What good did this do him? He stomped the curvy side of the period with his foot. "You're just a big fat dictionary, after all," he said aloud. "At least the other books could talk. What can you do?"

For a moment nothing happened. Landon sighed and shook his head. Then the book began to shake, and thunder rumbled overhead like the crashing of giant bowling pins. Landon flinched but held his ground. When the trembling stopped, an idea popped into Landon's head. It seemed as if the book *had* spoken to him somehow.

Turn the page.

Now the reason he would turn the page was—

Nah. Landon was tired of figuring out reasons. Right now

he just needed something to do. And standing on a period in the *Book of Meanings* wasn't it. Landon decided to turn the page.

Turning a page in a book is usually no difficult trick. As Landon looked about him, however, he realized this was no ordinary page and no ordinary book. This would require his whole body and some hard work. Landon took a deep breath. He'd come this far, so he was more than up for the task.

He was standing on the right-hand page. To his left, the page rose toward a peak, beyond which lay the middle of the book. Landon turned to his right and started to jog. It was quite a ways yet to get to the side of the page. As various black shapes passed beneath him, he pretended they were line markings of a football field. The bottom margin was the sideline. When he finally reached the right margin, he thrust his hands up and shouted, "Touchdown!"

The book rumbled lightly in response.

Landon went to the edge and looked over, then stepped back. It appeared to be an endless drop into darkness. Kneeling down and crawling to the edge, he took hold of the page with both hands and peeled it up and in. It lifted surprisingly easily—it was paper, after all—so Landon stood and began backing up, pulling it with him. Finally he turned around, gripping the page behind him, and began to run.

He was crossing the football field again, this time unfurling a vast American flag for the national anthem. An imaginary crowd cheered him on. Landon ran faster. Suddenly he was moving faster than his legs were actually propelling him. The page had gathered enough momentum that it was now pushing him across the field.

A wild idea came to him, and Landon leaped into the air. He was flying! Sailing with a huge cape gently rippling behind him. Down he came, his legs churning, and up he went again. This was better than jogging on the moon. He didn't even need a spacesuit. (Though the thin oxygen level was still in effect.) Dark letters passed beneath his feet in a blur. The ground was sloping upward. At the top, Landon could see the other side of the book spread like a creamy farm field with flat black shapes. And then he saw the valley below.

Oh no. Landon plummeted toward the middle of the book, a dark crevasse that dropped into the binding. His feet were sliding against the texture of the page. At the last moment, when he was sure he was to disappear between the pages forever, something happened. He was going up again. He was saved!

But Landon had a new reason to panic. He'd been so successful turning the page that now it was going to finish the job on its own. It was rising up and up, straightening out for the descent to the other side. The letters below that had appeared so huge were now recognizable. Landon could see sentences. Then whole paragraphs. Then the entire page became visible below. Soon the letters were almost too small to make out. This wasn't good.

Landon's arms were twisted backward. His shoulders felt wrenched from their sockets. His hands were sweating and losing their grip. *Oh, please, please, please.*

For a moment, it seemed he'd stopped moving, uncomfortably dangling high in the sky. Then he was moving again, back down. Landon's "Oh, thank you, thank you, thank you" soon turned to "Oh no, oh no, oh no." Yes, he was coming back down, and that was good. The bad news was that he was at the edge of the page. At the rate the page was falling, getting faster each moment, Landon would be flung from the book like a bug flicked by a giant finger. There was no time to come up with reasons. There was hardly time to think. As the paragraphs became sentences, and the sentences words, and the words let—

One of his hands slipped.

"Ayeee!"

From the blur of rushing letters below, he noticed one that seemed marked just for him. The letter *X.* Landon focused on it, and when it approached, he dropped.

Chapter Eight

As Landon fell toward the *Book of Meanings*, he thought, *Stop, drop, and roll.* By the time he realized that's what he was supposed to do if his clothing had caught on fire—not when he was falling into a book—it was too late.

"Aaah—*oomp*!"

His knees buckled, and his body collapsed like a telescope. But he did roll. In fact, he did a short tumbling routine that would have impressed the judges at a gymnastics meet. After his third somersault followed by a cartwheel and a jerky stiff-limbed handspring, Landon finished with a signature round-out belly flop. "Oof." Then he rolled over.

The sky was falling.

When someone says, "Don't panic," that means there's probably good reason to get anxious and excited and frantic about something. Though no one else was around, it was

as if someone had shouted it into Landon's ear, *Don't panic!*
So he did. Landon hopped right up and began to run like a
crazed rabbit.

There was nowhere to run to, of course, no escape. But
it hardly mattered. He couldn't take this lying down. An
odd cloud with a perfectly straight edge passed overhead and
zoomed toward the horizon. The page darkened. Landon
ran like Jonah trying to escape from inside the whale, but its
mouth was closing fast.

Swoosh!

A gigantic wave smothered Landon, burying him
facedown in what felt like sand. Everything was grainy
and dark. He couldn't breathe. It felt like a steamroller was
running over him, pressing him flat.

Suddenly, Landon felt a strange sense of peace, and he wondered if he had died. It was like he was no longer in his body.
He was someplace else. A great book was before him, lying open
on a stand. He approached the book and—taking the left-hand
page between his thumb and forefinger—turned a page.

What was this? Something fluttered out from between the
pages. Was it a feather? A dried leaf or a flower? No, Landon
realized as the object gently floated to the floor. It was. . .
him. How long had he been trapped between the pages? he
wondered.

The sand that had been so tightly packed around him
began to shift and loosen. Landon could move. And he could
breathe. *Gaaasp.* He was alive!

There was a strange belching, swallowing noise. Landon flailed his arms and legs, trying to grab hold of something. The sand had given completely away, and he was falling. Again.

Oh. . .no. . .

A cement floor came into view. Smack. Darkness.

It could have been a second or a minute or an hour or more. When Landon opened his eyes, he saw the rough surface of the floor stretching before him. He closed his eyes. The entire front side of his body felt plastered to the cement. Or perhaps *into* the cement. When he got up, he imagined he'd see an impression in the awkward shape of a sprawled crime-scene victim. But to his surprise, the floor was flat. He hadn't made a dent.

"Ohhh," Landon moaned and flexed his limbs. He was stiff and sore all over. Not remembering what had happened or where he was, he thought he might be waking from an outlandish dream. Looking around, however, he changed his mind and thought he'd just fallen into one.

Something popped and flickered and buzzed like a neon sign. It *was* a neon sign.

QUALITY.

That's what it said. A big glowing yellow word with all the letters connected by little tubes. There was some more fizzing and humming and blinking. QUALITY went out but just below it another word appeared.

CONTROL.

It was also bright yellow neon. When it went out a moment later, QUALITY instantly reappeared and then CONTROL again, and they flashed back and forth several times before both going dark.

QUALITY.

The sequence started all over again.

Now two more signs came to life, one on either side of him.

To Landon's left were the capital letters *A* and *M*, separated by a dash. They burned pinkish red, and beneath them was a door.

To Landon's right was another door, with the letters *N* and *Z* over it. The letters, again with a dash between, glowed blue.

Could it be chance, thought Landon, *mere circumstance. . .*

He was starting to remember what had happened and was working on where he might be, when another commotion caught his attention. Something was moving near the corner. It was rising from the floor with the whining *whirr* of a hydraulic lift. It looked like a ladder with a stool on top. It was a rising ladder-stool. In the wall to the right of the rising ladder-stool, an arched hole appeared—*swish!*—like a giant mouse hole. From it emerged not a giant mouse but a little man shaped rather like an egg. *Swish!* The hole closed up behind him as he tottered to the ladder-stool.

Plunk. The man hopped onto a rung of the ladder and began to climb, even as it continued rising. *Clink.* The stool finally stopped about five feet from the ceiling. The man continued to climb, and Landon had the impression he was

watching a circus performer going up for a high dive. When the
man reached the top, he sat on the stool, facing the back wall.
Landon heard another noise as something seemed to come out
from the back wall toward the man. *Clunk.* It stopped.

What a strange room, Landon thought. Though it was
empty save for the man on the ladder-stool and whatever was
behind him and the neon signs, for some reason it felt like a
warehouse. Maybe it was the concrete floor and the mostly
blank walls and the high, corrugated ceiling. Landon limbered
up his shoulders and arms and walked toward the ladder-
stool. He came alongside it and looked up. The little man sat
still as a stone. Before him was a rectangular block protruding
from the wall. The man's arms and hands were above the
block and out of view.

Landon felt a little dazed. Still, it seemed only polite to
try and make some conversation. He cleared his throat and
tested his voice. "*Ha ha hmm.* Hello there, sir!"

The little man came to life like an automaton, rocking
rhythmically back and forth as a series of *clicks* and *clacks* and
tippity taps sounded from above the block. Then he stopped,
and Landon heard a ripping sound—*zip!* The man stood atop
the stool, pivoted, and leaped almost straight out. His head
nearly brushed the ceiling, and he was gripping something in
his hand that trailed after him, rippling through the air like
the tail of a comet. It was a white paper banner.

When the man touched the floor, he took off at a fast
wobble for the door that appeared faintly red beneath the *A–M*

sign. He opened it and went through, the streamer snapping in after him as the door clapped shut. A moment later, the door reopened, and out came the man teetering and tottering his way across the room to the other door. *Snap, clap, shut.* He reemerged just as quickly and came waddling toward the stool-ladder. No! He was coming straight for Landon.

The banner had been rolled up into a scroll, and as the little, egg-shaped man approached, he held it out like a baton. He seemed to be offering it to Landon.

Landon stood spellbound a moment, helplessly staring. The man was even more peculiar close up. He wore a translucent green visor and a shiny black vest, like a banker in the Old West. His nose was disproportionately large and protruded from the middle of his face like a cucumber. His two eyebrows were black and bushy, and his one mustache was even bushier. It looked like a fuzzy, overgrown caterpillar that might crawl across his lip in either direction at any moment. Then there were his eyes. They blinked repeatedly as if in reaction to the electric hum of the neon sign. And they appeared a number of sizes too small for his head. They were either actually that tiny, or it was only the effect of the immensely thick lenses he had strapped to his head.

Landon forced himself to look away. Odd as the little man was, Landon did not want to offend him or appear rude. That's when he noticed the long wooden pencil perched behind his left ear.

The man waved the baton, and Landon started. *Oh yes*, he

thought, reaching out to take it. As soon as the paper was in Landon's hand, the little man turned, squatted with his elbows back, and jumped. It was such a swift springing motion that Landon felt sure he had just witnessed a grasshopper take-off. When he glanced up, the man was already sitting on the stool, facing the wall, his hands over the block. Motionless.

Landon began to unroll the scroll. He saw in large capital letters *HA HA HMM* printed across it. He crouched and laid the paper on the floor to open it all the way. The rest of the banner read, *HELLO THERE, SIR.* Then Landon noticed something else. Beneath each typed word were some handwritten words done in pencil. He glanced up at the man sitting statuelike, the writing instrument jutting from his ear like an antenna. Landon sighed. This was strange.

Beneath *HA,* the little man had apparently written "vocal utterance used interjectionally to convey alarm or as a reaction to something funny. See 'HA-HA.' " Under the second *HA,* an arrow pointed to the definition below the first. *HMM* was defined as "a humming sound hummed interjectionally between thoughts or while pondering." *Hmm,* Landon thought to himself, being careful not to make too much sound.

For *HELLO,* the little man had penciled in, "Noun, vocal utterance used when meeting or in addressing another person in person or over the phone. May be used interjectionally to convey alarm." *Ha,* Landon thought, though he didn't say it out loud. Hmm, that one big word—"interjectionally"—

showed up a lot. How on earth had the little man written all this down in so short a time?

THERE was defined, "Adverb, denotes location, may be uttered interjectionally"—there it was again!—"to convey smugness, tenderness, agreement, completion, or resistance."

And finally, *SIR.* "Noun, title for a baronet or knight, deferential term of salutation for a male person or personage."

Landon liked to know the meanings of words, but this was almost more confusing than clarifying. And that one word that kept showing up, what did it mean? It didn't make sense to define a short word using much longer words. Before he realized what he was doing, Landon was sounding it out loud. "In-ter-jeck-shun-al-ly. Interjectionally." And then he heard the typing sounds.

Clickity tappity clickity.

A ripping noise was followed by the little man soaring through the air, paper in hand. Down he came and off he went, to and through the red door. *Swish, snap, shut.* In a blink, the door opened again. The little man came waddling over to Landon, handed him a very thin scroll, and then pivoted and popped from the floor like an exploding kernel of corn.

Landon could open this scroll while standing, though it nearly stretched the length of his arms. The printed word was that big. It was kind of funny seeing a banner with the word *INTERJECTIONALLY* on it. But Landon didn't say, "ha" or "ha-ha," he merely read the hand-scribbled definition. There were two definitions, actually.

"One. Having to do with an interjection." Well, that certainly didn't help much. "Two. A parenthetical remark or word without the parentheses. A word or gesture adverbially tossed amid other words or gestures."

The more Landon read, the more confused he became. Finding a simple meaning for something wasn't proving very simple. All these words were beginning to give him a headache. Then he thought of something. *Could it be chance. . . ?* The Auctor's Riddle. It was all coming back to him. He had turned the page. And he'd wound up here. He set the second—and completely pointless, if you asked him—banner on top of the first on the floor. His shadow faintly flickered from the flashing QUALITY CONTROL sign overhead. Landon looked up at the little, egg-shaped man. (How could he sit so quietly?)

"Auctor. Riddle." Landon spoke clearly and deliberately, and immediately the little man set into motion like a ticking machine. Though Landon couldn't see it, he deduced there was a sort of typewriter up on the block. A typewriter that stamped large letters sideways. It sounded like a toneless music box.

Landon heard the paper rip and watched the man sail down like a comet. He rapidly waddled to the red door first and then out and across to the blue door. He hadn't yet rolled the paper, so it rippled behind him between the doors like a banner trailing an airplane. *"AUCTOR RIDDLE."*

Landon received the paper with interest, hardly noticing as the little man pounced to the top of the ladder-stool like a spring-loaded cat. What did *Auctor* mean anyway? He was about to find out.

"Noun. Latin for creator, originator, producer, composer, author."

Landon felt his stomach flutter and a tickle run up his spine. He now knew four Latin words: *porticus* (porch), *ex* (from), *libris* (library), and *auctor*. The two words were similar. The Author's Riddle. But who was that? Did the author write the riddle? Or was it a riddle about the author?

The scribbled definition for *riddle* actually made sense. Landon felt good that he could understand it. "Noun. A puzzling series of words to be sorted, pondered, and possibly solved. A profound or mysterious question. An enigmatic enquiry."

Landon suddenly had the urge to leave this curious place. If the little man wasn't using the stool-ladder, Landon could climb it and, stepping on the block, test the ceiling. That had been how he'd entered the room, wasn't it?

Of course, there were the two doors. Landon glanced at the motionless man and started walking toward the blue door. Something made him pause, and he turned and looked. The little man had spun round on his stool and was glaring at him. Landon gulped. He could try to make a dash for it. But he had seen how fast the little man moved. There was no way he could outrun him. What would the little man do to him, though? An uneasy feeling made Landon not want to find out.

Looking at the floor, Landon shuffled back toward the

banners. When he glanced up, trying not to lift his head, the little man was facing the back wall again. Weird. Landon sighed. Apparently a frustrated exhalation of air didn't count as a word. The little man didn't move. Landon breathed again, loudly, in and out. He looked up. Nothing. How would he escape?

Wait a second. Perhaps gasping and panting didn't make the little man flinch. But what if he heard something that *sounded* like a word, even if it wasn't? Landon mulled this over for a minute. Finally, he was ready. He took the deepest breath of his life, held it, and then—

"Zhoozamazamadooeyrammadooeydooeymannaflooey-sillyflammyrammygammy. . ."

In Landon's excitement he ran out of breath early. But it had worked! The little man teetered furiously atop the stool, rocking to the sound of toy machine-gun fire. *Tappity rappity tappity pappity rap!* Landon leaned on his knees, a base runner ready to steal second. He could actually see the paper curling up and over along the ceiling like an extended receipt curling from a cash register. Rip! And here comes the pitch!

The little man leaped from the stool, landed lightly on the floor, and then he paused. The banner undulated after him, gently falling to the floor like the tail of a Chinese parade dragon coming to rest.

The little man fingered his way down the paper, pausing now and then to glance up, blinking at Landon. Landon held his breath, poised and tensed. He couldn't take this much longer. The little man tilted his head and, with a bewildered peek at Landon, seemed to shrug. Finally he turned for the blue door, slowly wobbled his way over, and touched the doorknob.

The little, egg-shaped man took his time opening the door. But once he was inside, the streamer slithered surprisingly quickly through like an electrified tapeworm. *Snap, clap, shut.*

Landon was so tense that he'd become nearly rigid. For a moment, he couldn't move, petrified and terrified the little man would return before he'd managed to escape. *Come on, legs!* he wanted to shout. Finally they responded, and Landon took off—in seemingly slow motion—toward the red door. He saw the glowing red letters above him. *A–M.* He fumbled with the doorknob. *Come on, come on!*

The door opened. Landon stepped inside. Before him stretched a long corridor. He started to run. A door appeared on his right-hand side. He ran past it. Farther on, another door appeared, and then still farther on, another one. Landon was about to slow down as he passed the next one, at least enough to give it a good glimpse before flying by. But just then, he heard a door slam far behind him.

Landon ran and ran. Where was the end of the hallway? It was lit by bare bulbs dangling from the ceiling. Though he dared not slow down, something on the next door caught his eye. It was a letter. As the next door approached, Landon noticed the letter *C.* He sprinted on, his eye grazing the wall for the next door. There it was. The letter *B,* which could only mean that the next one must be—

Something was behind him. Gaining on him. Light footsteps and huffy panting. Landon glanced at the door. *A*—he was right! He couldn't resist. He turned his head to look behind him.

Chapter Nine

Landon never saw what—or who—was chasing him down the hallway. At the moment he turned his head, just after passing the door with the letter *A* on it, he tripped and careered onto the floor.

This floor proved very different from the rough concrete of the corridor, however. Whatever it was made of, it was smoother and slipperier than glazed ice.

As Landon slid on his pajamas like a human torpedo, he wondered if perhaps it *could* be ice. Then he decided it couldn't be for the simple fact that it wasn't cold.

So this was what it was like before the beginning of the alphabet. A vast slippery floor. The little egg-shaped man and the Quality Control room slipped quickly into the background. If that had been the little man chasing him, well, Landon was pretty sure he wouldn't catch him now. Plus, he had a feeling the man never left the room or the two hallways except to go into his mouse hole.

Boy was he sliding fast! Landon wished there was something else to think about other than how slippery the floor was and how fast he was skimming it. He pictured lugers and bobsledders and speed skaters and downhill skiers, knowing he must be moving faster than any Olympic athlete could ever dream of.

Eventually, gradually, little by little, in a not-sudden-or-abrupt way at all, Landon began to slow down. Somewhat. A while later, he was still slowing down. And some time after that, when his speed had been reduced to perhaps that of a world-class cross-country skier, Landon pressed his hand to the floor to produce drag. But this only set his body spinning, which he immediately regretted.

He couldn't stop spinning, and he might throw up at any moment.

Landon had experienced something like this before when he was six and a big, mean kid of seven or eight had made him stay on the merry-go-round when he'd been more than ready to get off. The mean kid kept pushing the bars, sending Landon around and around. When the monster's mother finally came to Landon's rescue, it seemed the earth had been permanently tilted. Landon had tried to walk straight home, but he'd kept going sideways and stumbled over a bicycle lying on the grass. When Landon eventually made it home, he didn't throw up, but he was sure he would never eat another peanut butter and jelly sandwich again.

The sliding was going slowly now, and the spinning was easing into a leisurely rotating movement. Then Landon stopped. He closed his eyes and rested a bit, waiting for his brain and body to realign with the universe. When he thought his equilibrium was stabilized and that he wouldn't be sick, he tried to stand.

It didn't happen. His feet slid apart like repelling magnets. The floor was *that* slippery.

After banging his knees, an elbow, and his rear end, Landon gave up.

He sat on an endless floor. Everything beyond the floor was lost in whitish haze.

Which direction had he come from? There was no hint of the corridor that led to the Quality Control room. No indication of any page or book or library. Absolutely nothing was visible. Landon knew deep within his gut what it meant to be lost—in the middle of nowhere.

It wasn't time to panic, he thought. Not yet. Give him, oh, at least another minute or two—

"Help!" shouted Landon. "Help! Help! Help! I'm stuck out here!"

Landon noticed something. Beneath the glossy surface of sheer smoothness, the floor was composed of large squares. Landon was sitting in the center of one himself. It had the look of dark, deeply polished wood. Adjoining his square on each side were much lighter squares, also wood. It was a giant checkerboard. Coffee- and cream-colored. And here he was smack in the middle of it.

"Mate in seven moves!"

Landon glanced up from the floor. Some distance away stood a towering figure. It appeared to be some sort of statue. Broad at the bottom and then tapered upward toward two collar-like rings, and then slightly flared again toward a flat top. Flat, that is, except for a square-shaped cross jutting up. It was dark brown in color—very similar to the color of Landon's square.

"Did you say that?" asked Landon. "What *are* you?"

The figure came sliding toward him, then stopped.

"Mate in six moves."

The voice, low and resonant, seemed to come from nowhere and everywhere at once.

"Wait a second, hold on," said Landon, not sure what—or who—he was talking to. "What do you mean, 'Mate in six moves'?" He tried to mimic the deep bass voice. "I don't under—"

"Mate in five moves." The voice spoke louder as the figure slid closer.

The wood figure was so large and tall that when Landon realized what it was a shiver ran up his spine. Of course, it was a giant chess piece—the dark king—and the squares that lined the floor must mean Landon was on a vast chessboard.

"But I'm *not* a chess piece," Landon explained. "You can't put me in checkmate. I'm just an innocent bystander"—he looked at his position on the floor—"well, by*sitter* anyway."

The dark king advanced, oblivious to Landon's counter. "Mate in four moves," the rumbling voice bellowed.

Landon felt a bit nervous. Perhaps if he explained how he had arrived here and that it wasn't his fault, the king would leave him alone. Was it his fault? How *did* he get here? The looming presence of the dark king disrupted Landon's thinking. His mind was drawing a blank. Let's see. He had slid out here from the corridor that led to the Quality Control room where he'd met the strange little egg-shaped man. Before that, Landon had been on the *Book of Meanings* where he'd been caught after turning a page onto himself. How had he gotten up there?

He'd been climbing. That's right. What an experience that was. And did he remember a news reporter interviewing him from a helicopter? Hmm. Anyway, he knew he'd been climbing the side of the book a good long while.

What else? Oh, yes. Yes, oh. The speaking books in the library. That was a fanciful conversation. And before that? Of course, the Auctor's Riddle, Part One, on Bart's gravestone. Did that mean there was another part to the riddle? He wondered why he hadn't thought of that before.

Still further back was the dreadful dark tunnel—oh, skip that part. Too nasty. Landon had found it by going down the stairway from his grandfather's study. . . .

Grandpa Karl. He'd been hurt. There was an accident. Was he all right now? Landon hoped so. He remembered lying on the sofa and hearing thumping from outside. Perhaps this would be a good place to start explaining.

"I was in bed, right?" said Landon. "Well, actually it's my grandpa's sofa *made up* like a bed. Anyway, I was thinking about the library—the BUL, you know. It was the middle of the night, when suddenly I heard—"

The dark king bellowed. "My trusty steed, my knight! Yes, he should be here to witness his king's conquest."

Landon trembled. One giant chess piece was more than enough, thank you! "No," said Landon. "That's not what I meant. I meant it was dark outside—a dark night." He heard how that sounded. "No!" Landon grimaced and shook his head. "Not a dark *knight*. I didn't mean. . ." This was hopeless. How could he distinguish "night" from "knight"? Now he'd really dug himself a hole.

But if Landon had been inside a literal hole, he'd have jumped right out at the king's next command.

"Knight!"

The word shot like a firework into the air and exploded in every direction. Landon flinched and covered his ears. He imagined an onrushing stampede of mammoth pieces. Pawns and bishops and rooks surrounding him and closing in. Landon had heard that if he felt anxious about a situation he could calm himself by finding something humorous about it. For instance, to give a speech in class, he could pretend his classmates—and teacher—were puppies panting or monkeys scratching their heads.

Landon made himself look at the dark king. It stood quietly, which was nearly as disturbing as seeing it move and hearing it speak. Landon couldn't picture it as a dog or a monkey. But it did share a certain resemblance to an oversized lamppost. Or a lighthouse. Or a huge candlestick holder. *Or even,* Landon thought, tilting his head, *a funny-shaped upside-down birdbath.*

Out on the horizon, something moved. It looked like a bouncing dot. Whatever it was, it seemed to be speeding across the board—toward Landon.

The dot grew into a blurry dark object that was not merely bouncing up and down but was also skipping from side to side. The movement was mesmerizing. Rhythmical. Landon found himself counting—*One-two-three, one-two-three*—at first silently, then, unable to contain himself, right out loud. "One-two-three, one-two-three, one-two—"

"Mate in three moves!"

The king slid closer. Landon stopped in mid-count, his mouth puckered on an "ooh" sound. The dark bouncing blur—bigger around than the king though not as tall—abruptly halted a few squares away. It was a dark brown bust of a horse. *The knight.* Its chiseled eyes stared blankly over Landon. Its teeth were etched into an eerie grin.

Landon glanced between the pieces. No one spoke. Nobody moved. Finally in a small, glum voice, Landon said, "I don't want to play."

"Mate in two moves."

Scarcely breathing, Landon said, "I want to go home." He couldn't pretend the king was a funny birdbath or a lamppost. There was nothing funny about this. Landon only wanted to curl up into a ball and disappear from this gloomy place to wake up safe and cozy in bed.

The voice wasn't loud or deep or booming. It spoke with such a soft, sickly sweet rasp that Landon's skin crawled. It seemed the voice was next to him, gently blowing into his ear. "Mate. . .in. . .one. . .move."

Landon didn't have to look up. The king's massive base filled the square ahead of him. Landon knew he couldn't stand and run. There was something he hadn't yet tried, however. Crawling. He rubbed the floor's surface. It might be even too slippery for that. His knees would slide back while his hand shot forward, leaving him flat on his stomach again.

This triggered another idea. What if he were to lie on his stomach and low crawl, as he'd seen soldiers do in war movies? It was more like slithering than crawling, really, and it was certainly worth a try.

Being careful not to utter a word or sound and so provoke the king to make another move, Landon lay back and rolled over to his belly, and then he tried to crawl. It felt almost as if he was climbing the *Book of Meanings* again except he wasn't making any progress. He was moving his arms and legs, but it was like trying to swim against the current in a river. He was going nowhere. Finally he tried to hunch up his body like an inchworm and throw himself forward. After three desperate lunges, he had moved about an inch.

He would never get off this square, let alone across the board. Landon sighed miserably. The king and the knight loomed behind him, waiting. Landon sensed their horrible presence without looking back. They would probably wait forever while Landon struggled futilely on his square. And then, when he made a noise or said a word. . .

Well—then what *would* happen? Landon looked at the endless floor before him. Even if he could walk or run, which he couldn't, it would take forever to reach the horizon. What he needed, he thought excitedly, was a good *push*.

Of course! It seemed so obvious to him now. The giant king would glide right onto Landon's square, bumping him and sending him flying across the board! The king would get his checkmate and Landon would be moving again, quite possibly toward some escape. It might hurt, getting rammed by that massive figure. But what other option was there? Landon could think of none.

Landon arched his back and lifted his head. "Okay, Great King," said Landon, his heart beating madly against the floor, "come and catch me if you can!"

Landon wriggled and struggled vainly, but it was mostly for show. He made two quick inchworm lunges, going nowhere in a hurry. It felt good to move, he was so anxious and excited. He had to release his nervous energy. He was half wincing and grimacing at nothing, expecting the impact from behind any moment. Finally he stopped, panting, and wondered why nothing had happened. "Okay, King!" he taunted in singsong. "Come and get me!"

A voice seemed to come from high in the air. "Chehhhck!"

Landon craned his neck to look behind him. There was the knight, staring and grinning hideously. But where was the king?

"Maaay. . ." The voice from above grew louder. And what was that other noise? It was like a whistle. Like an incoming mis—

Landon arched his back and lifted his eyes. A dark circle came his way.

Chapter Ten

I t is difficult to describe exactly what happened next. Landon knew he was going to be squished like a bug. He thought of his mom and dad and sisters and grandparents and wondered if Grandpa Karl was okay and wished that he were home with all of them. Landon was so paralyzed by fear and so sure he was going to die that by the time he understood he was not dead nor squished like a bug, well, then something else was already happening.

Solid wood jammed his body. Landon closed his eyes, fearing the worst. But he was not slammed from above. He'd been hit from the side and somehow hoisted upward, and then he was rolling in midair. Before he could wonder what he was doing up there, he was jarred again—*thump*—this time from below. Landon reached out to grab something—anything—and his hands came upon two angled ridges of wood. Though he'd never ridden a mechanical bull, it seemed he had landed on one now. The wood form beneath him bounced and reeled at warp speed.

Landon opened his eyes. "Whoa! Whoa! Whoa-whoa!" The words were bumped right out of him as Landon bounced against something hard. The coffee- and cream-colored squares of the floor were passing below in a joggling blur. What had happened? What was going on?

There was a violent quake, and a voice rumbled. "Traitor! Betrayer! Outlaw knight! You are hereby banished from the game! Forever!"

Landon flinched. The quiet following the thunderous rant would have been eerie had he not been struggling to hold on to this, this. . .

The knight. Landon was on the back of the dark wood horse head. The knight! They were hopping a herky-jerky course away from the king. Landon was saved! Tears moistened his eyes. He would never again take it for granted that he was three-dimensional. But why had the knight saved him? Was there a reason? It hardly mattered. Landon was alive. The least he could do was thank his rescuer. But speaking between the lurching jumps would be challenging. They were moving so quickly.

"Thank you, Mr. Ho–orse!" said Landon. "I mean, Sir Kni–ight!" Boy, this was tiring, just getting the words out. Landon tried to catch his breath.

"You're welcome, my friend."

It talked. The knight could speak through that clenched grin. Its voice was surprisingly calm and soothing. Not at all like the bellowing king. "I'm sorry about the bumps—not much I can do about it. Are you okay back there?"

"Y–yes," said Landon happily. "I'm o–ka–hay."

"Good," said the knight. "The king was not playing by the rules. I have secretly despised him ever since he first neglected the code."

Landon's knuckles ached. He was trying not to slide off.

"To take advantage of an outsider," said the knight, "and a helpless one at that. Well, that was too much. I could not stand idly by and let that happen. Banishment or no banishment."

Where were they going? Landon wondered. Did the board go on forever? Were they just fleeing the king temporarily? Wait a second. What was that in the distance? Through a shifting haze, pillars and high arches appeared, but then they faded. When they became visible again, Landon felt an odd mix of excitement and dread. Beyond the arches was. . . nothing. They appeared to mark the corner of the board.

"There are two of us, you know," said the knight. "Two dark knights to do the dark king's bidding. When I heard him beckon, I knew that I must heed this call. And I am glad that I did. But now that my duty is done, I'm afraid, so is my life. For I have been banished from the game."

The knight spoke clearly and evenly despite their bounding from square to square. Not only did his voice not break, his tone also did not waver. It was monotonous or flat, like a boring teacher Landon had in the third grade. The knight didn't come across as dull, however. Through the wood Landon seemed to sense something. Beneath its grim exterior and the calm droning voice, the knight seemed somehow—sad.

"Why–y. . .are. . .you. . .ba–an–nished?" asked Landon.

Hop hop, skip. Hop hop, skip.

"For treason," said the knight. "I am a knight of the dark color, and I have betrayed the dark king. We began our quest on the same side of the board, and I had always moved on his behalf. Until now. Now I have moved against my king, and for that I am rightly being banished."

The white columns and arches at the corner became clearer. They ran only so far in either direction along the edge of the board and then stopped. Perhaps they were leftover ruins from a former wall or structure. Landon's feelings of dread and excitement were leaning more toward dread. Beyond the arches lay nothing but dreary fog. They were trapped. Landon might be stuck here in nowhere forever.

They reached the corner square—a creamy colored one—and stopped. Just like that, the rocking ride was over. A distinct cadence kept repeating in Landon's head: *one-two-three, one-two-three, one-two-three.* The rhythm of the hops. Landon tried to let go of the knight's ears, but he couldn't. His hands had seized up, becoming as hard and wooden as the horse head itself. Landon looked at his hands as if he could unlock them with his eyes. They appeared not to belong to him. He couldn't feel them, and they looked like white bird's claws.

The knight remained silent. A new panic arose within Landon. What if the knight never spoke again? The panic gave way to an acute loneliness. Landon didn't want to lose his only friend here. He was finally able to lift one finger, and he used it to tap the knight's ear. "Hello? Sir Knight?"

"It is time for you to continue on with your journey," said the knight. "I know not your mission or your quest, but be assured, I wish you well."

Landon was dumbfounded. Continue with his journey? What journey was he on? What was his quest? *Could it be chance. . .he wound up on this chessboard? Mere circumstance?* "The Auctor's Riddle," Landon said softly. But where could he go from here?

The fog swirled and swept over the corner of the board. It crept along the outer edge like ghostly fingers.

"You may step off here at the corner," said the knight.

They stood on the corner square, beyond which lay a dark brown border perhaps twenty feet wide. The pillars rose from the border. The arches loomed overhead.

"What did you say?" Landon asked, shaking his head. The haze seemed to be seeping into his mind. "Did you say 'step off'?"

"I believe you will be all right," said the knight.

Landon wasn't so sure. Jumping blindly into vaporous froth did not strike him as a great idea. He could move his fingers again, so he lifted his hands. Ouch. They throbbed as the blood rushed into them.

"What about you?" Landon asked, stalling. "What are you going to do?"

Landon thought he heard the knight sigh, or maybe it was a sudden gust spilling onto the board.

"I will wait here," said the knight. Landon again sensed a trace of sadness. "I am not made for life beyond the board. This is my world. I will await the consequences for my actions. It should not be long."

Consequences? Wasn't he already banished? What more could the king do? "Well, can't you just stay away from him—or it—the king?"

"The king? Oh, yes. No problem. His movement is limited to one square. The queen, however—she is a big problem. For her, the only limits are the borders of the board. She may travel freely in any direction at great speed. From her there is no escape."

The queen? You mean there are other chess pieces on the board? Where are they? Landon suddenly had a very uneasy feeling about this. He swallowed and slowly turned to look behind him. The knight seemed to be thinking the same thing. It began to pivot, and Landon grabbed hold of the ears, his hands instantly finding their places again. The vast scope of the chessboard came into view.

A figure appeared far in the distance. As it drew nearer—at an alarmingly fast rate—Landon could see it was similar in shape, size, and color to the king. But it wasn't quite the same.

And then the knight said, "She's coming to complete my banishment."

Landon could only stare and swallow. Somehow it seemed she might also be coming for him. Suddenly the thought of stepping off the corner didn't seem as bad an idea as it had a minute ago.

"You had better get off now," said the knight, as if to affirm Landon's thoughts. Landon had noticed the first time the knight had mentioned the queen its voice had actually fluctuated. This time there seemed a very faint tremor. Was the knight afraid, too? Its next comment was back in the flat, staid tone. "Carry on with your quest and fare thee well. I shall stand fast to meet my fate."

Landon was tempted to run. He did not want to meet the queen. His fingers released the knight's ears, and he thought about sliding down its back and sprinting to the corner. Or at least hiding behind a pillar to see the outcome.

No. He couldn't do it. He couldn't leave the one who had saved him at the risk of its own, well, banishment.

"How do you know you're 'not made for life beyond the board'?" asked Landon. His own voice sounded amazingly calm, he thought, considering that his heartbeat was accelerating. "Have you tried it?"

"No. Now please, go."

"Not unless you come with me." Landon spoke firmly, though his insides had turned to jelly.

The knight said, "But my punishment—"

"You did what was right," said Landon. "You protected me from the king, and you shouldn't be punished for doing what's right. Right?"

The knight was silent. The queen would arrive in seconds. There was no time to argue.

"Now," said Landon softly, trying a new tack. "Now you can protect me from the queen."

It worked. Appeal to a noble steed (the head of one, anyway) with a noble deed. The knight almost seemed to straighten its neck and lift its jaw. It was more a sense than any actual movement. "Protect you from the queen," said the knight. "Protect you from the queen. This I will do."

They spun back toward the arches. Landon sensed something extraordinary was happening as the knight hopped tentatively forward. One. They were off the square. Off the chart of the board. He hopped again. Two. They were under an arch. Thankfully, there was enough room to the left or right for a side-hop, which is what the knight took next. Three. The next two forward hops took them to the very corner of the board. From here a hop in either direction would send them over the edge, into the mist.

The knight stalled.

Landon squeezed its ears and nudged its neck. Why weren't they moving?

"If I am to be banished from the game," the knight said slowly, "then I might as well remove myself from the board. Young lad—"

"Landon. My name's Landon." *Come on, Knight! Let's go!*

"Young Landon, if I should perish from this feat, do not pity me. I am doing my duty. For that I am glad."

Was that a siren wailing from behind? Landon was afraid to look—in any direction. He closed his eyes. "Okay," he said, "let's go on the count of three, all right?"

"On the count of which number?" said the knight.

The siren had become a shriek. The board began to tremble like a track beneath a roaring locomotive. Or was it the knight that was shaking? Landon squeezed his eyes shut tighter. "Three," he said, tensing. "Three!"

Landon braced for impact, but it didn't come. The knight had leaped to the right. And then there was nothing but a great, upwardly rushing wind.

Chapter Eleven

Landon's pajama legs and sleeves rippled and snapped in the breeze. His hair seemed to be flying off his head. He opened his eyes, but there wasn't much to see. The haze was thick, veiling him and the knight in gauze. Something was happening, however. Landon could feel it.

The first things he noticed were the knight's wooden ears. They had become soft as velvet and fit entirely inside his hands. And they had started to twitch—no longer much to hold on to. Landon slid his hands from the ears to some long, coarse hair. The knight's solid neck had softened and changed shape as well. It was still firm but not like wood—more like powerful muscle. Landon laced his fingers through the hair and clutched it toward his chest. And that's when he heard a startled whinny.

Landon then noticed his pajamas had stopped flapping.

He could feel a tough, burlap-type material wrapping his legs and a shirt hugging him that was heavier than his pajama top. Some sort of footwear covered his feet, though he couldn't see it, and there was little wiggle room for his toes to explore.

How long had he and the knight been falling? It was difficult to tell. When the milky haze suddenly lifted, Landon winced at the bright light. Then he looked up. Above him loomed a magnificent cloud. A great distance below lay the earth, the world—a canvas of browns and greens spread in every direction as far as the eye could see.

Landon shouted over the wind. "Are you okay, Sir Knight? You look different now. I think you're a horse!"

The horse's skin was twitching and tugging all over the place. "Everything itches and tickles!" it said, whinnying and snorting and jerking its head.

"Whoa! Easy!" Landon squeezed his legs and pulled hard on the mane. "It's just your new skin!" he said, and then he almost laughed because that sounded so funny. New skin! Speaking of which, Landon surveyed himself to check out his new duds.

His shirt was off-white and speckled with light brown dots, though they weren't dirt, just part of the fabric. It felt like he was wearing a belt, which he couldn't see. And his pants were a deep tan, tapered and tucked right into his tall dark boots. He had boots! He *looked* like he should be on horseback, Landon thought happily. The clothes certainly weren't modern, however. They were like the garb a boy would wear in medieval times, a boy who took care of a knight's armor and the knight's horse. What was the word? *Squire*, that was it. Landon Snow the squire. And he had a knight and a horse all in one!

Landon's cheerfulness didn't last. The sight of his clothing and the transformation of the knight had distracted him from the gravity of their situation. They had just dropped from a cloud and were plummeting toward earth.

With no parachute.

This was really too absurd. How could anyone fall to earth on a horse? Had it ever been done? What Landon needed to figure out, and quickly, was how it might be done successfully. That is, how could he land and live to tell about it?

There was no water below. At least he didn't see anything blue. It was all greens and browns. Landon thought back to his crossing of the *Book of Meanings* when he had soared over the valley—the book's middle abyss—holding one page and then falling to the page below. He had simply collapsed and tumbled and rolled. But that didn't seem like such a good idea for this situation. What if they could somehow hit the ground running? If there were some sort of downhill slope that they could catch at the right angle, well, it could be like landing on a ramp after a motorcycle jump.

The ground was rising much too fast. Actual treetops became discernible. Landon scanned the topography for what he was hoping to find, his eyes watering against the whistling wind. "Can you move your legs?" he shouted even though the horse's ears were only inches away.

The horse flung its legs out awkwardly and then brought them back in. It was not a very encouraging display.

"Good," Landon said, tapping the horse's neck with his clenched fist. "That's our landing gear." He gulped down his fear and tried not to cry, though his eyes were already streaming liquid. He tried to ignore the voice inside his head that screamed, "We're dead, we're dead, we're dead!"

"I see a ridge," said Landon. He tugged the horse's mane to the right. "There it is." One side of the ridge appeared quite steep and disappeared into a broad thicket. *It's too short,* Landon thought. The other side was a long, gentle slope. *A perfect runway,* he thought excitedly. But then he noticed the far end of it. The slope ran to the verge of a cliff. There was no time to consider other options. They would just have to slow down enough to stop before plummeting over the edge. The thought of landing from the sky only to go plunging over a precipice didn't hold much appeal.

Landon leaned forward and to his left, guiding the horse toward the long side of the ridge. He shouted into the horse's ear. "As soon as we touch down, start running as fast as you can!" Meanwhile the little voice was hollering, "Dead meat, dead meat, dead meat!"

Well, maybe so, Landon thought, *but at least we are going to give this amazing landing experiment a shot.*

The ridge looked like raised scar tissue on the earth. As the jagged line rose quickly to meet them, Landon pulled back on the horse's mane to slow their descent. The horse whinnied and jerked its head, and Landon eased up a little.

"Sorry," he said. This landing was not going to be gentle. Just before impact, every muscle tense, Landon shouted, "Start run—" He bit his own sentence short as they struck the stony surface.

Landon's face crashed into the mane, and he flung his arms around the horse's neck. They were charging down the slope but not in a straight line. The horse was lunging this way and that every three steps as if racing through a slalom course. Bits of rock and clods of dirt flew in either direction as they zigzagged steadily downward. Landon held on as he bounced back and forth. What in the world was the horse doing? Dodging invisible trees?

Through the dust, Landon could see what lay ahead of them. Nothing. The ground came to a stop. They were headed for the cliff. Suddenly Landon brightened. Of course! The horse was doing its crazy gallop in the same pattern as it had hopped on the board. And the back-and-forth motion could very well be slowing them enough to save their lives. The rhythm was even there—one, two, three. . .one, two, three—though here it was broken by a skidding, rock-scattering turn between each count.

The ride ended. The horse panted and snorted, but he had stopped running. Landon's arms had stiffened round the horse's neck. He blinked through the settling dust, and when he saw just where they were standing, his grip tightened another notch.

The cliff fell two feet away. Down below, *far* down below, stretched a vast green valley. Across the valley in the distance rose bluish-gray mountains, preceded by brown and green bumps, the foothills. About midway between the cliff and the mountains snaked a silvery river, leisurely winding its way through the valley.

The green of the valley looked like plush carpet from this height. Or like different colors of moss. Some dark patches, some bright lime, and many shades between. Cloud shadows passed slowly over the landscape. Landon lifted his head and turned to look back up the slope. He could no longer tell which cloud they had fallen from. An armada of large, puffy clouds floated through the sky.

He patted the horse's neck while still clinging to it. "Are you okay?" Landon said, thinking of the horrible jolt the horse's legs must have endured upon landing and then the beating they took scrambling down the rocky slope.

The horse began saying, "That was—"

It started and shuddered and whipped its tail about. For a moment Landon feared it was going to suddenly jump right over the edge.

"Exhilarating!" the horse finished, stamping its hooves. "I think I'd like to try that again!"

As the horse turned and cantered and seemed readying to rear up, Landon yanked on its mane. "Whoa, no!" he said. "Easy, easy. Let's take a minute to figure this out."

The horse wagged its head and snorted but didn't seem

too bothered by Landon pulling its mane. It was prancing in a circle, sort of pivoting about like a high-stepping dog chasing its tail. Whenever the valley came into view, Landon squeezed tighter and closed his eyes until it passed. It was a bit dizzying.

"What's there to figure out?" asked the horse. It stopped rotating, and Landon breathed a huge sigh of relief. Then the horse started going in the other direction.

"Well," Landon said, closing his eyes and then opening them again. "For one thing, we need to figure out how to get down there"—he peeked at the valley through one squinted eye and then snapped it shut—"from up here."

The horse stopped, faced the valley, and walked to the very edge so that its head and Landon's were hanging over. Landon buried his face in the horse's mane.

"Why not just step off," said the horse, "as we did from the board? I believe that was a far greater descent than this appears to be." It pawed the rocky rim eagerly, and Landon could hear bits of stone crumbling away.

"I know, I know," said Landon hastily. "That was different though. Now we're back on earth, or someplace like it, and the rules here are not the same. I mean you can't just jump off a cliff. It doesn't work."

"How do you know?" questioned the horse. "Have you tried it?"

Landon sighed. He had the feeling the horse was using the same reasoning on *him* that Landon had used to convince the knight to jump from the corner of the board. "No," said

Landon. "But I just *know*. There's gravity here, and laws and rules that if you break them, or try to break them, well. . ." He thought for a moment.

"Well, what?"

"Well, then they might break you."

"Oh," said the horse, though Landon didn't think it sounded too convinced.

"Could you just back up a little bit, please?" Landon pleaded. He could feel a cool breeze rising from the valley and hear it whispering past his ear. He seemed too high up to actually hear it, yet something in the wind seemed to suggest a rustling from countless leaves down in the forest.

The horse snorted. "All right. If it will make you feel better, young Landon. But how do you know so much about the laws and rules here?"

The horse took a step back. More earth gave way beneath its hoof. This caused its leg to buckle, and Landon lurched a foot closer to the valley. He bit his lip to keep from screaming. When they had retreated a few more paces, Landon finally breathed and then let out a long slow moan. He loosened his grip and sat up. He surveyed their more immediate surroundings. "I know the rules here because this is where I'm from."

The horse lifted its head. "You come from *here*?" It sounded astonished. Its voice range must have expanded as part of its transformation from wood to flesh. The monotone was gone.

Landon didn't recognize where he was, other than that

it appeared to be earth or something like it. It seemed a very familiar world after the *Book of Meanings* and the Quality Control room and chessboard. The cliff made him think of the Grand Canyon, and the distant mountains brought to mind the Rockies, though he hadn't actually seen either of those formations with his own eyes. Only in pictures. In fact, he'd hardly traveled anywhere outside Minnesota before. There were no deep canyons or high mountains in the state—though it had many beautiful rivers and lakes.

Landon cleared his throat and wiped grit from his mouth with the back of his sleeve. "Well, I've never been here specifically. Let's just say this place looks sort of like my *board.*"

The horse lowered its head. "I see. So on this board, how does one get from a high place to a low place without jumping?"

Since Landon claimed this was his board, he now felt responsible to know everything about it, which he didn't at all. How does one get from a high place to a low place without jumping, or using stairs, or taking an elevator, or climbing down a rope or a ladder?

"I don't know," said Landon. "We just have to look around and see if we can find some way down."

He guided the horse to the left, being careful to keep several feet between them and the edge of the cliff. He didn't want the horse to get any funny ideas. Since they were still operating on two different boards, as it were, Landon couldn't fully trust the horse's judgment. Though the horse certainly didn't seem to have any ill intentions.

As they wandered along, looking for a possible way down, Landon glanced over at the valley now and then, and across at the mountains. It was a breathtaking view.

The sky gradually dimmed, and the clouds had moved toward the mountains and beyond. Landon gauged the mountains were to the north, as the sun glinted from the far end of the valley. The mountains themselves softened to a faint purple and began to fade in the dusk. Darkness was creeping up on them from behind. Landon shuddered, remembering the vapors clambering at the edge of the chessboard like ghostly fingers. A yawn welled up inside him and seemed to climb out his mouth, stretching it wide. The easy ambling of the horse was lulling him to sleep. He began to wonder as if in a dream whether they might be stuck up here. So far there was no indication of a path or trail that could lead down to the valley.

The sun surrendered its glare as it sank toward the far end of the valley. But something else flashed at the corner of Landon's eye. He straightened up, alert. *What was that?* He steered the horse close to the rim and then pulled back on its mane.

"Whoa. I think I saw something down there." Landon scanned the distant scenery, but it was getting dark. It was hard to distinguish between the shades of green. "Did you see anything?"

The horse turned its head toward the valley, but it seemed to be listening more than looking. Its ears twitched inward and then outward again.

Landon could only hear a light breeze that whisked up from the depths. He saw the flash again. "There it is!" Pointing excitedly to a place about halfway from the cliff to the river, Landon noticed it wasn't a momentary glimmer but a series of flickering lights from one spot. A second later it had stopped, and the valley was dark. He couldn't look away. It seemed there was a circle around where the flashes had occurred. He strained his eyes, trying to capture it through the darkness. When he blinked, he lost sight of it.

"I heard it again," said the horse.

"What? You heard what again?" But then Landon said, "Wait. Look! The light!"

The dot of light flickered from the same spot as before, and then it disappeared. The sun had melted to a thin orange line at the valley's end. The orange line turned pink, then blue, purple, and finally black. Stars dusted the sky. The river had become a silvery thread.

Standing near the cliff's edge in the darkness was not a good idea, Landon decided. He coaxed the horse away, nudging him to step to more solid ground. Against the blackness of the chasm, the line of the cliff was discernible thanks to the starlight. As Landon's eyes continued to adjust, he could see well enough to be safe. Everything was in black and white or, more accurately, in shades of gray. His plan would simply be to stay away from the line of the cliff for the night.

The excitement of the flashing light faded, and Landon yawned. He remembered the horse's comment. "You said you heard something? What did you hear?"

"Hmm. I'm not exactly sure. I'd never heard it before. To describe it, I would say it was the sound of a thousand voices. Possibly more."

A thousand voices! How could Landon not have heard that? He glanced at the line of the cliff and beyond. "What were they doing?" he asked. "I mean, what did they say?"

"Hmnph." The horse snorted. It seemed to be thinking again, perhaps trying to figure out how to describe what the voices said. "It sounded like the letter *O* and something else. Like this: 'Ohhh-whoa.' "

"Ohhh-whoa?" said Landon. *Ohhh-whoa. What on earth did that mean?*

"Do you want to keep going? I think I'm losing my eyesight," said the horse.

"Ohhh-whoa," Landon said without thinking. "Yes. I mean no." He pulled the horse's mane and then eased up. "I think we should stop here for the night. I'm getting ti. . .ai. . ." Landon yawned and stretched. "I'm getting tired. If you can't see and I can't stay awake, well, I don't want to fall off this cliff."

Landon brought his right leg stiffly over the horse's back and slid to the ground on the side opposite the cliff. It felt strange to be standing. His legs tingled, and his feet felt prickly. He realized he hadn't been upright since he'd run down the corridor from the Quality Control room and then tripped and slid onto the giant chessboard.

Landon admired the noble creature beside him and patted

its flank. "Thank you," he said softly.

The horse pleasantly shuddered and snorted. "What for?"

Landon sighed and thought for a moment. "For doing your duty," he said. "And for saving me twice."

"Ah, well, for that I am glad. You are welcome, young Landon."

Weariness was filling Landon's body like sand in a sandbag. He let his knees give way, and when he sat down, it felt delicious. The ground was hard and rocky, but Landon knew he would have no trouble falling asleep. He was about to lie down when he saw the sign.

How had he missed it before? It was sticking up from a pile of rubble almost right in front of him. There was a wooden post holding a large square board with words on it. The letters were dim, the light was even dimmer, and Landon's eyelids were drooping by the moment. But he wanted to see what it said. Using his remaining energy, he scuffled forward, closer to the sign.

The words appeared one on top of the other.

Everything went dark.

Landon couldn't keep his eyes open. This was harder than trying to read a boring book for school. Landon's head fell forward and actually bumped the sign. This startled him awake momentarily, and then his eyes closed.

He had seen something, though. The top word. *The. Come on,* he told himself. *Two more words. You can do it.* He forced his eyes open. *Weigh.*

Darkness. *The Weigh. . .*

His body jerked, and he lay down. Oh, sweet ground, sweet rest. But somewhere deep inside, he knew there was something he wanted to know, something he needed to see. His eyelids fluttered, and he saw it. A sign loomed over him. The bottom word was *Down.*

As Landon drifted into a deep slumber, three words floated through his brain. Somehow, even in his sleep, he knew he had found The Weigh Down.

uring the night Landon dreamed he was on top of a cliff. Of course that's where he was. And in his dream there was a sign nearby, just like the one jutting from a pile of rubble near his snoring body. But in his dream, the sign said, FOR SALE. And then: DANGER. Yet again it said, WATCH FOR FALLING BOYS ON HORSES. Landon giggled in his sleep at that one. It was outrageous. He dreamed he walked around the sign to find a poem printed on the back. Though the poem seemed familiar, it caused him to toss and turn on the rocky ground as he read it. It went like this:

> *Could it be chance, mere circumstance*
> *That man eats cow eats grass eats soil*
> *And then man dies, and when he lies*
> *To soil he does return?*

Landon saw green blades shooting up from the dirt and then a cow's mouth snatching them and chewing and then a man sitting down to a big juicy steak dinner and then the man had a heart attack and fell over and he was buried in the ground beneath the dirt and green blades were sprouting above him. . . .

That dream was interrupted by another in which Landon was waking and looking up at the stars. There were the Big Dipper and Orion. And a bright dot that might be Venus.

But what was this? Above Venus (if that's what it was), a short line of stars glimmered, then one by one formed a swooping curve like a sickle. Other stars dimmed until this new formation was the brightest in the sky. Landon nearly hyperventilated from excitement. This was a discovery of astronomical proportions. He would become famous and go down in history as the boy who discovered the constellation Question Mark.

Something was snorting and snuffling and slurping nearby. Landon feared the cow was back eating grass. . .and making its way toward him. Landon wiggled his fingers and rolled his head. He wanted to say *moo* and *move* and *blech* all at once, but what came out as he suddenly swiped at the air over his head was a resounding, "Melech!"

"Good morning, young Landon."

Landon opened his eyes, sat up, and blinked. A horse was licking a small pile of stones around a signpost.

"These taste good." Slurp, slurp. The big dark tongue

seemed to be a creature all its own. Landon made a face and turned away.

"Did I just say something?" Landon asked. His dreams were already fading, being replaced by the waking reality that seemed just as fantastic. The cliff, the sign, a beautiful, dark brown, talking horse. . .

The horse lifted its head, its tongue still flicking. "You said, 'Melech.' " Its muzzle opened when it spoke, and Landon noticed its healthy teeth.

The teeth. A memory rose as if from a dream, but Landon knew it was true. He saw a giant chess piece knight, a wooden horse head with sharp ears, blank eyes, and carved grinning teeth. *That was you,* Landon thought in amazement as he watched the horse. "Melech."

The horse nodded. "That is correct."

An idea came to Landon. "Do you have a name?" he asked.

"A name? Well, I used to respond to 'knight.' Somehow I understood when it referred to me and not the other. But a name, hmm, I suppose not."

"Would you mind if I called you Melech?"

The horse lowered its head and then raised it. "Not at all, young Landon. This former knight would be honored to be so dubbed." It bowed its head and bent one knee. Landon felt his face grow warm with both humility and pride.

"Then Melech it shall be," he said, and he patted the black crown of Melech's head.

Melech whinnied, and Landon laughed with him. They both

paused and grew quiet. Landon swallowed and glanced around. He cleared his throat. "Well," he said finally. "How 'bout this sign then. It says, 'The Weigh Down.' What do you think?"

"I think it's a grand idea," Melech said with sincerity. "What does it mean?"

"That's just it," said Landon. "It's spelled wrong for what it sounds like it means." Did that make any sense? This would be hard to explain. "If it said The *Way* Down—W-A-Y—then I'd think there would be a path or secret stairway or something. But The *Weigh* Down, I don't know."

"Well, what does this word mean?" said Melech.

"It means. . .well. . ." Landon tilted his head. "It's to see how heavy something is."

"Hmm." Melech flared his nostrils and sighed.

Landon's body felt stiff and sore. He stood and raised his arms and rocked his body from side to side. He looked at the sign. Then he jumped up and down. A little dust arose; otherwise nothing happened.

"If only there were another sign to explain this one," said Melech thoughtfully.

Landon paused. He pointed at Melech and then at the sign. "That's it," he said. "The other side. . ."

Landon stepped around the sign. Whereas the front had three large words, the back was littered with little ones. "My goodness," muttered Landon. "Somebody wrote a book back here." Curiously enough, it actually looked like a poem.

"Oh, and I heard it again," said Melech.

Landon looked up from the sign. "Heard what?"

"The sound from last night, a thousand voices."

A chill ran up Landon's spine. "You mean the 'ohhh-whoa' sound?"

Melech nodded, his ears twitching like antennae. "Precisely. I heard it three times, and then I could see again."

"You could see again?"

Landon looked to his right, toward the east. The sun had just cleared the far end of the valley. The night's shadows were being burned away by the rising of the day. "Ohhh-whoa," said Landon. He looked back at the sign. They *had* to get down to that valley!

Black powder was stuck on the board to form the words. It reminded Landon of art class in school when the kids drew on paper with glue, dumped glitter over it, and then lifted the paper so only the glue-stuck glitter remained. Landon leaned on his knees to study the small, fuzzy letters:

> *The weigh down is the way down*
> *The place where two ends meet*
> *A journey ended here*
> *Would be a journey incomplete*
>
> *It seems so far away*
> *From here to there from high to low*
> *Some tools will prove handy then*
> *To help you as you go*

These words you see are not just words
Just rub to find they're soot
Stand quite still, crouch right down
And trace around each foot

That is for the human boy
No soot for the horse will do
Bigger longer two more legs
He's taller and heavier too

Take the signpost from the rock
Use it to carve four grooves
Into the stone and into which
The horse may place his hooves

Landon read it twice, the second time carefully noting what he was supposed to do. It seemed strange—rubbing soot? Tracing his feet? Carving grooves?—but what other option did he have? He cupped his left hand, held it against the board, and with his right hand began wiping down the letters. They fell surprisingly easily. There was no glue. Somehow the soot had managed to stay put until he brushed it.

Soon the board was blank, its back message dissolved. A wave of panic ran through Landon. What if he forgot what to do? He should have read it aloud to Melech to help him remember. Feeling a sneeze coming on, Landon covered the black dust with his right hand, cupping the precious contents.

After two soft explosions through his nose, he scanned the ground for a flat spot where he could go to work. The best place was near the cliff's edge.

Landon cleared away scrabbly bits of brush with his foot. He crouched down and blew at the ground. When the stone looked clean, he began dabbing his index finger into the ash and tracing around his boots. The breeze from the valley tousled his hair, but he tried not to look down. He had to concentrate until he was finished, making sure the outlines were complete before relaxing his left hand and then wiping both hands on his pants legs.

"There." Landon stood and felt the blood rush into his head. He closed his eyes. When he opened them, the sight of the drop before him nearly made him swoon. He realized he'd locked his knees, reluctant to step from his freshly drawn footprints.

"Are you all right, young Landon?"

Melech's voice helped bring him back.

"Yeah," Landon said, flexing his knees and carefully stepping back toward the sign. Now what was he supposed to do? Something about carving. . .but where? And with what? Landon looked around helplessly. He felt lost.

"Are you going to do that for my feet as well?" offered Melech.

"Yeah," Landon said slowly. He was supposed to carve around the horse's hooves, with the signpost. But how could a wooden post carve into stone?

THE WEIGH DOWN. These letters didn't brush off. In fact, they looked as if they'd been printed on the board years ago and had faded over time. Landon grabbed the board from beneath and tried to lift. A jab of pain shot through his legs and back, which were still stiff from lying all night on rock. The sign didn't budge. It was stuck like the legendary sword in the stone. Perhaps Landon wasn't worthy to remove it.

He tried again and again, straining and groaning. Pain cut across the palms of his hands where the edge of the board had impressed a sharp crease. "Ugh!" Landon said, letting his arms droop and shoulders sag. He panted. A bead of sweat rolled from his forehead to his eyebrow. He blinked. "I can't do it," he said between breaths. "It won't come out."

"What does the sign say?" said Melech.

"The Weigh Down," said Landon. Hadn't he told him that before?

"Hmm."

Landon looked at him. " 'Hmm' what?"

"Well," said Melech, "if weigh means to find how heavy something is, and down is down, I'm wondering why you are trying to lift it up. Merely a casual observation."

A drop of sweat tickled Landon's nose and then fell to the pile of stones Melech had been licking earlier. He stood still a moment, wondering if Melech was playing with him. But really he was wishing he had thought of it himself. Here was a horse that may have figured something out on Landon's own board before he did.

Harumph.

Landon rested his fingertips along the top of the sign. " 'I'm wondering why you were trying to lift *up*,' " he muttered to himself, "when it clearly says, The Weigh Down."

"What's that?" said Melech.

"Nothing."

Landon glanced at his companion. The horse really did appear to be merely casually observing. With a sigh, Landon pressed down with his fingers. The sign sank so quickly, Landon nearly tumbled right over it. A soft click sounded, and up came the sign again—launching like a toy rocket.

Landon caught hold of the post and found himself walking backward with the sign over his head. The cliff was back there somewhere, but he couldn't stop. Then, *bump,* something stopped him. Landon turned. Melech stood on the very edge of the precipice. Landon stepped forward unsteadily and lowered the sign. "I thought the sign really was going to take me down the fast way." Landon's heart was still pounding.

"I heard the rules here are different," said Melech, side-stepping in from the edge. "The law of gravity and all that. I thought it best to prevent your falling."

"Thanks. What's that now, three times you've saved me?"

Melech snorted. "I have done my duty and am glad for it." He seemed to be smiling.

Landon smiled. "I'm glad, too."

The bottom end of the signpost was not wood. It was heavy steel that shone brilliantly in the sun. And it tapered to a fine, sharp point. *So it would be useful for carving after all,* Landon mused.

Melech was standing in a good spot right where he was, several feet away from Landon's boot prints. The blade scraped into the stone as if it were leather. When Landon tapped it or accidentally whapped the board against Melech's hindquarters ("Sorry," Landon said each time), the steel end rang like a tuning fork. Laying the board aside, Landon inspected each hoof ring for breaks. Satisfied, he rose, brushed his hands, and went to stand in his own two boot prints. He looked expectantly at Melech, though for what he didn't know. Several minutes later, Landon put his hands on his hips.

"Well, this is exciting," he said sarcastically. "Did I leave something out?"

Melech's ears twitched. "The sign," he said, nodding toward it.

"The what?"

"The sign," said Melech. "You left it out."

Something inside Landon burned. Was Melech playing with him? Or was this merely another casual observation? "You take everything so literally, don't you?" Landon meant this as an accusation more than as a question.

"Well, I don't see why not," said Melech.

A gust of wind caused the sign to teeter against the stony ground. Landon stared at it, fighting the urge to go and put it back into its slot. *Left it out. What did a horse know?* Finally Landon laughed and shook his head. He stepped out of his prints and picked up the sign. "This doesn't mean you're smarter than me," he said, glancing slyly at Melech.

"No, of course not," said Melech. He sounded so sincere.

Landon kicked away some pebbles, found the opening, and gently slid the signpost into the ground. The world seemed to become unnaturally still. Even Landon found himself holding his breath as he tiptoed back to his boot prints. He placed his left foot, and then his right, and the world was still no more.

Chapter Thirteen

Anyone who's been in an avalanche knows the helpless feeling that comes when the ground suddenly and totally gives way beneath one's feet. Then there's the feeling of having one's stomach fly right into one's throat. This, of course, is accompanied by a great desire to grab on to something—anything—to maintain one's balance and to keep from falling any farther.

Somehow Landon did maintain his balance, or at least he stayed upright, though it was in no part due to his skill at maintaining equilibrium. He really had no choice. The ground did give way beneath him, and down he went. But he went with it, not apart from it. It was like descending on a huge, open-air elevator that moved at precisely the same speed as an eleven-year-old boy would plummet. In essence, it felt like Landon was pushing the whole cliff down to the valley by merely standing on it.

The Weigh Down indeed.

Melech, being heavier than Landon, might have been experiencing similar sensations. Who could tell? He seemed to be taking the whole thing in as a casual observer.

And then, it was over. Landon's stomach dropped from his throat to his ankles, and he wobbled and stumbled forward and collapsed. Gritty dust settled everywhere. Landon choked and coughed and sputtered and spit. Then he sneezed twice and looked up. The forest was magnificent.

Landon crawled onto the grass, which felt like plush carpet.

The trees appeared taller than seemed possible. Landon, still on all fours, craned his neck like a howling wolf, his mouth open but silent as he gazed in awe. Finally Landon lowered his head and crawled farther onto the grass.

"Come try this," he said, patting the grass. "You've never stepped on stuff so soft."

Melech sniffed tentatively and then walked onto the lawn. He whinnied immediately and lowered his head again. His tongue darted out. "It tastes soft, too, after those salty rocks."

Landon looked at the grass and licked his lips. Nah. He wasn't that hungry. As he crawled (it really felt good to be on all fours here) toward the trees, he noticed bushes beneath them. On the bushes were berries. Big, dark, and blue.

Landon's mouth watered. He crawled faster. Plucking one with no thought for his own safety (strange berries might be poisonous, of course), he popped it into his mouth and moaned with satisfaction. It was the sweetest and juiciest blueberry he'd ever tasted.

"Melech, mmm, try these. They satisfy your hunger and your thirst."

Melech bared his teeth and gums and bit one berry from the bush. A guttural sound rippled from his throat.

"Good, huh?"

Melech chomped three more—*snip, snip, snip*—and chewed vigorously, his jaw working in a pedaling motion. "Young Landon, these are magnificent. To have existed before was simply not to have existed."

Landon laughed. He was sitting on the grass and had eaten more than his fill. He wiped his blue-stained fingers on his pants and looked up at the canopy of branches and leaves. A bubble formed in his belly and climbed quickly into his throat. Landon opened his mouth and belched. He laughed again. "Excuse me."

What Landon heard next caused him to nearly jump from his skin. A rumbling bullhorn of a blast erupted beside him. Landon stared, wide-eyed, and Melech turned and stared right back, equally amazed. "Pardon *me,*" said Melech. Then they both laughed, though Melech's sounded more like a whinny.

It was time to explore the forest.

They hadn't wandered too far among the trees before Landon noticed something strange. He found no signs of any animals or insects. No birds singing, squirrels rummaging, flies, gnats, or bees buzzing. The forest was eerily quiet, save for the gentlest of breezes stirring the leaves. It didn't feel dead, not with the thriving trees and plants and golden-green sunlight filtering through. It only felt. . .empty.

"I think we're the only ones here," said Landon. Something made him not want to speak too loudly.

"Are there supposed to be others?" said Melech.

"I don't know," said Landon. "I don't know."

His footsteps and Melech's hoof-falls seemed amplified with no background noise to absorb them. *Crunch, crunch, snap, crunch, crunch.* Something caught Landon's eye. Movement up ahead. *Is it a butterfly?* he wondered, his heart leaping. He stepped quickly. *Crunch, crunch, crunch.* Where had it gone? He looked around and then up into a tree and then down at the ground. Ah. This was what he'd probably seen. The forest floor was littered with helicopter seeds. Landon was standing under a maple tree.

A helicopter landed in his hair, and he pulled it out. Why was he afraid to speak up in a deserted wood? "I don't know where we are or where to go. Maybe we should try to find the river."

Melech stood still as a hunting dog pointing toward a hidden quarry. Only his ears moved. He seemed to be listening.

Landon lowered his voice. "What is it?" He glanced around warily. A few more helicopters fell, spinning silently. Landon looked up. A pair of eyes glinted high in the tree. One of them disappeared, the other one squinted. *What in the world?*

A stick seemed to pop up from the earth near Landon's

feet, scattering winged seeds. The top of the stick had feathers attached to it. As Landon studied it, he had an odd feeling he was being watched. Fear began to paralyze his legs and grip at his heart as he peeked back up at the branches.

"Bombs away!" a piercing voice shouted. Limbs and leaves began shaking, and Landon was blinded by a blizzard of twirling helicopter seeds. They whirred around him and tangled his hair like a swarm of locusts. The voice screeched, "Intruders! Trespassers! Violators! Ingrates!"

Another feather-topped stick seemed to burst from the ground about a foot away. The voice shouted, "Nuts! Rats!" Landon knew the stick hadn't sprung from the ground, however. He looked at Melech. "He's shooting at us!" he said. Then, realizing he couldn't move his legs, Landon cried, "Melech, help!"

Melech lowered his head and pushed Landon out from under the tree from behind. An arrow landed nearby. "Climb on," said Melech.

Somehow Landon managed to clamber aboard. He squeezed Melech's flanks with his legs, leaned close, and took hold of his mane. "Let's go," Landon whispered, unable to raise his voice. "Let's get out of here."

"Say no more, young Landon." Melech reared slightly with a whinny and took off through the forest. When he abruptly cut to the left or right to dodge a tree trunk, Melech reminded Landon of his slaloming gallop down the slope. But his one-two-three rhythm was gone. He was certainly no longer a knight on a chessboard but a stallion on a mission. His mission? To get away from whatever was shooting at them!

The arrows kept coming, zipping past on either side or sailing overhead. Whoever was shooting sure had decent range and a lot of arrows, but fortunately he was not a highly skilled marksman.

"Nutcrackers! Rattlesnakes!" the shrill voice shouted after them. After three more misses, it called again, "Ratchet! Nutmeg!" But with each powerful stride Melech made, the voice faded farther behind.

The forest was quiet again, yet still the arrows were coming. Landon couldn't believe it. They must have traveled at least a mile. They darted from a tree, and an arrow split it just behind them: *Thunk!* Incredible. How many arrows did that thing have? And just how far could he shoot? It was impressive, but it was getting a little annoying.

After another mile or two—it was hard to gauge distance zigzagging through a thick forest—the arrows finally stopped. Landon sat up. Melech slowed to an easy canter.

"I want to say that was close," Landon said, glancing back, "when actually it was pretty far. I wondered if that thing would ever give up, whatever it was."

"I guess we were not alone, after all," said Melech.

Landon pondered this and looked at the trees around them. He saw no more eyes peering back at him. Melech seemed relaxed enough. He breathed a sigh of relief. "Do you think we're heading toward the river?" Landon asked. "I can't even tell where the sun is from in here."

The trees were so tall and the leaves and branches so thick that though there was plenty of light—in a glowing, dappled sort of way—it really was impossible to see much of the sky at all.

"I'm not sure about the river," said Melech, "though it appears we may be headed toward something else."

"Would you look at that," said Landon, staring. "That tree is *huge.*"

The tree's trunk was so large a small army could be hiding behind it, and Landon would be none the wiser. And because the tree was so enormous, it wasn't until they were right up on it that Landon noticed something else. Attached to the giant trunk was a board.

"And look at that." Landon pointed in amazement. "Another sign. Whoa, Melech. Let me take a look."

Landon dismounted and went to the board. It wasn't much of a sign. All that was on it was a circle with a hinge across the middle. The top half of the circle was blue with a shiny gold disk. The cogs in Landon's mind turned as he worked to figure this out.

"Maybe this is the sky, and that's the sun." He pointed at the disk.

The hinge across the middle held a wooden flap that was swung downward. Landon lifted the flap and pushed it up over the blue semicircle on top. This revealed the bottom half of the circle, which was all black.

"Aha!" said Landon. "Black as night." He raised and lowered the flap as the rusty hinge groaned and creaked. "Interesting." Then Landon paused and peered at Melech. "Did you say something?"

Melech shook his head and then stopped, his ears upright and alert. Landon listened, too, and turned back toward the tree. Stepping to the side of the day/night board, Landon took hold of two ridges of bark and leaned in as closely as he could with his ear. The tree was making noises. It sounded like it had indigestion. Suddenly, the sound changed.

A rhythmic thumping, not like a drum but like footsteps trodding wooden stairs, came from within the trunk. Then they stopped. Something began to click. *Click, click, tick, click, tick, tick.* Landon winced as a horrible wrenching sound filled his ear. When the tree began to move, he jumped like a startled rabbit.

Landon bumped into Melech and took several more steps back. The tree wasn't moving. It was opening. A large section of the trunk had swung outward. As Landon stared, breathless, a figure emerged from the tree.

Chapter Fourteen

The figure strode over to Landon, waving a finger and making a *tch-tch-tch* sound. Landon thought it was going to poke him right in the nose, but then it pivoted on its heel and went to the sign. The flap was up, showing the bottom black half of the circle. The figure briskly lowered the flap and pointed at the gold disk. Without turning around, it lifted its finger and said, "Sun up!"

At first Landon thought he might be looking at a gnome. The figure looked like a shortish plump man wearing blue coveralls and a pointy red cap that drooped. But didn't gnomes live in yards and gardens, where they came to life at night when no one was looking? This thing came from inside a tree, so maybe it was an elf.

Something was strapped to the elf's back, and Landon realized with alarm that it was a quiver full of feather-topped sticks. A curved stick with a string swung from a clip on its hip. A bow. Landon swallowed. Without taking his eyes from the elf, he began moving slowly toward Melech. When he had his hand on Melech's flank and was about to hoist himself up, the elf turned and glared.

"Sun up!" it said, pointing at the sky. It placed its hands on its hips. *"Tch-tch-tch-tch!"* The bow swung casually at its side.

"I'm sorry," said Landon, lowering his leg. "I won't touch it again."

The elf narrowed its eyes, darting them between Landon and Melech. Finally it thrust out its jaw. "Hmnph!" It began to stomp back toward the tree door.

"Should we perhaps ask for directions to the river?" said Melech.

Landon hesitated only a moment. "Wait!" he said. "Could you please—"

But the elf hadn't gone back inside the tree. With a swift kick, it had set the door in motion. The chunk of bright fibrous wood and thick rough bark swung back around and in, closing with an earthshaking *whump.*

The elf faced Landon and Melech, unclasped its bow, and reached over its shoulder to draw an arrow. Landon felt his knee begin to tremble as the elf fitted the back of the arrow against the bowstring and slowly raised it to eye level.

"Please, don't shoot, Mr. Elf. I meant no harm. We come in peace. I won't touch the sign again. We didn't know. . . ."

The elf had closed one eye, sighting up the arrow. It

wiggled its hips, causing Landon to blink and flinch, but then it slowly lowered its bow. "Eowf?" it said, looking perplexed. "No Mizder Eowf. Awd!" It let go of the bowstring, shooting the arrow harmlessly into the dirt—*plick*! The elf jabbed the front of its blue coveralls with its thumb. "Awd. No eowf."

Landon looked at the arrow in the ground and the empty bowstring. He breathed a sigh of relief. But then the elf was reloading, and Landon's knee began to quiver right where it had left off.

"I think," said Melech slowly, "that he's saying he's not an elf. He's an *Awd.*"

Landon's knee paused and then resumed its rapid shudder. "An Awd? But what is—"

The elf—or Awd—had another arrow pointing in their direction. Without Melech to lean upon, Landon probably would have fallen right over in a faint. He could barely stand as it was. Somehow Melech seemed to be remaining calm and unaffected despite their adversary's taking aim at nearly point-blank range. The Awd swiftly moved, and Landon collapsed like a bag of potatoes. But even as he fell, he noticed that no arrow was flying in their direction.

Melech's nose nuzzled Landon's ear, and the effect was like smelling salts. Landon grimaced and raised his head. Then he stood up. "I'm awake, I'm okay," he said, as if he had to convince somebody. "What happened?"

"He shot the other way," said Melech.

"What?"

The Awd was off to one side of the tree trunk. It glanced back, saying "Echo echo green green. Dreckshun." Then it drew out an arrow, fit it, raised the bow, and fired it into the treetops.

"I think he's trying to tell us something," said Melech.

"Was that the second arrow he shot?"

"The third."

Landon peered at the dense treetops and then as far ahead along the forest floor as he could. It was impossible to tell where the arrow—or arrows—had gone.

"What do you think that means, 'Echo echo green green'?"

"Perhaps it's a place," said Melech. "And he's showing us where to find it."

The Awd seemed to have overheard their conversation. It turned, nodding and waving the bow back toward the direction of the arrow's flight path. "Dreckshun! Echo echo green green!"

"How far in that, uh, 'dreckshun'?" Landon pointed.

The Awd grinned, revealing a less-than-full set of crooked teeth. "Twin-tee," it said.

"'Twin-tee'? You mean twenty?"

The Awd dipped its head, throwing the red point of its cap forward. It came back up. "Twin-tee."

Landon looked at Melech. "Do you know how far that is? Twenty. . . ?"

Melech blew air through his nose. "On the board I would think twenty squares. Here in the forest—how does one measure one's movement from place to place?"

Landon glanced at the Awd. "Twenty yards? Twenty meters? Twenty miles?"

The Awd leaned like a robin listening for worms, frowning. Then it popped upright and raised its bow as if to direct an orchestra. It swung the bow toward the tree, paused, and gently tapped it. *Tick tick.* "Twin-tee!"

It was Landon's turn to lean and frown. "Twenty. . .tree? Twenty *trees?*"

The Awd threw up its hands and danced a jig. "Twin-tee tree! Twin-tee tree!"

But Landon wasn't overly thrilled. He could count twenty trunks from where he stood. Beyond that the forest didn't look any different. The Awd paused in mid heel-to-knee position and glanced at Landon. Balancing like a ballerina, the Awd followed Landon's confused gaze to the forest, and then back again. It lowered its leg. "No, no," it said. It tapped the tree again with the bow. It spread out its arms as if to hug the tree. Then it gaped up, looking at the tree. "TWINNN-TEE," it said in a husky voice.

This giant tree was bigger than twenty other trees put together. What was the Awd trying to say? As if reading Landon's mind, Melech said, "Twenty like this. Twenty of this type of tree."

Landon thought of the tree opening and then closing with a *whump*. He nodded and began to feel tinges of excitement and nervousness. There were more colossal trees! Which meant

LANDON SNOW AND THE AUCTOR'S RIDDLE

there might be more Awds with arrows inhabiting them. Landon stepped forward, almost within reach of the red-capped Awd. Landon touched the tree. "Do you mean twenty of these? Twenty, uh, Whump Trees?" He patted it tenderly.

The Awd looked at him, its eyes glowing, and Landon knew he had his answer. "Twin-tee," the Awd said and pointed with the bow. "Dreckshun." It whipped out an arrow and shot it through the trees. The arrows vanished almost instantly, and Landon tried to picture its trajectory in his head.

"Thank you, Mr. Awd," Landon said, feeling a little funny. "Melech and I will be on our way then. Echo echo green green."

The Awd drew back as Melech approached. It seemed fascinated by him and a bit frightened. It studied his legs and body and tail and neck and head but only from several feet away. When the Awd abruptly pointed at Melech, it was the first time Landon had seen Melech start. Melech neighed and twitched his tail, seeming restless and anxious all of a sudden.

"Aminal," said the Awd. "Must see Ludo. Ludo must see."

Landon glanced back and forth between the Awd and Melech, not sure what was going on. What or who was Ludo? For some reason, he didn't want to ask. Why was Melech so uncomfortable? His jaw was clenching and unclenching as if he were chewing something. He was strangely quiet except for the soft, restless neighing.

"Okay, I think we're going now," said Landon. He patted Melech's flank and neck. Melech bowed ever so slightly, and

Landon climbed onto his back. Nudging him with his heels, Landon said, "Here we go. Twenty Whump Trees that away."

Melech bobbed his head and broke into an easy saunter. Landon glanced back, relieved to see the Awd wasn't raising another arrow and happy that they were leaving him.

"Is something wrong?" Landon asked. "What happened back there?"

Melech made a murmuring, neighing sound, and for one terrible instant Landon was afraid his friend was never going to speak again. "I do not know what happened," said Melech, and Landon sighed despite himself. "But I have a grave feeling that I am not welcome here."

They walked along. When the next giant Whump Tree slipped into view, Landon tried to feel excited, but all he could think about was how eerily quiet this forest was. . . because there were no animals.

They traveled at a leisurely, thoughtful pace until they reached the tenth Whump Tree. They were giving the trees extra-wide berths, partly because the trunks were so enormous but also because neither Landon nor Melech had any desire to arouse more Awds with arrows.

By the eleventh Whump Tree, however, Landon found his spirits lifting. They were over halfway to the mysterious echo echo green green. Landon wondered if it might be a cave or a canyon of some sort, places he associated with echoes. As for green green, well, this brought to mind the short bright lawn for putting on a golf course.

From a distance, the nineteenth Whump Tree appeared to be wearing an undersized apron of some sort around its vast lower trunk. Curious, Landon wanted to investigate. They approached to see a tall banner made of thick, leathery paper, secured by frayed lengths of rope that pulled the corners with fist-like knots. Beautifully scripted black letters stretched across the vellum:

Beware the one who seems not young or old
He will betray your trust
You have been foretold

Beware the lure of shimmering gold
That turns the mind to rust
And the heart to mold

Beware, my friends, do not be misled
The Odds are against you
They may want you dead

Not much of a welcome, Landon thought. Was this another riddle? It seemed so long ago that he'd read the riddle on Bartholomew G. Benneford's gravestone. *Could it be chance,* Landon wondered, *that this banner happened to be tied to the nineteenth Whump Tree?* Who else would see it here? If it was meant for him and Melech, what could it possibly mean?

"What does it say?" asked Melech.

"It's a warning. . .let me see. . .about someone who doesn't seem young or old, about shimmering gold, and about the Odds who may want you dead. Or maybe *us* dead."

Melech made a swallowing sound. "Should we turn back then, or head in another direction? This does not seem to be a very safe place."

But Landon hardly heard him. He was staring at something around the bend of the trunk. Or rather, at *four* things that were stuck into the ground about thirty feet away.

"Melech. . ." Landon mindlessly tugged at Melech's mane. "Look, Melech, over there—"

"But if this is a warning, young Landon, perhaps we ought to—"

"Melech."

The horse reluctantly turned from the sign, and Landon urged him away from the tree. In the ground were four precisely placed feather-topped sticks, each cutting the earth at the same angle. Landon dismounted and crouched to run his finger along one of the feathers. It was a strange feather that looked gray at first glance but then appeared to reflect a rainbow of color when disturbed. What sort of bird produced such a fabulous—

"Young *Landon*!"

Melech charged, sending Landon tumbling. Landon was about to yell and cry that Melech had nearly impaled him on the back of an arrow when he noticed the reason for Melech's behavior. A fifth arrow had landed ahead of the formation of the other four. Landon stared at it, his mouth agape. He looked at Melech, who simply stood with his ears pricked, always at the ready. The treetops through which the arrow had so recently flown appeared unruffled and nonchalant.

"How. . . ?" Landon began. "Where. . . ?" He gazed down at the five arrows, though he stood safely to one side. "So how many times have you saved my life now?" He didn't look up.

"Young Landon, I have done my duty and am—"

"I know, I know. And you're glad for it." He softly cleared his throat. "Of course, I am, too. Otherwise I wouldn't be here." Landon glanced up almost shyly. It was getting to be a little painful, being so indebted to another—to a horse—for repeatedly looking after him. How could he ever make it up?

"If my sister Holly were here," Landon said, "she'd know." He laughed. "She'd know exactly how many times we've done everything. And she probably would have counted not only the Whump Trees, but every tree we've passed so far."

"Your sister?" said Melech.

"Yeah, I have two of them."

"Hmm."

Melech was quiet, and Landon wondered if he even understood what a sister was. When Melech spoke again, however, he said, "About that sign, if it is there to warn us of something. . ."

Melech's voice faded as Landon realized what he'd been staring at the past few minutes.

"It's a connect-the-arrows...arrow!"

The five arrows piercing the ground did indeed form a picture of one big arrow. There was a point, two arrowhead corners, and a short shaft.

Landon smiled and shook his head. "For some reason I knew I didn't have to worry about another arrow shooting at me. Because he was just making this." Landon pointed at the five arrows and then followed the direction they were pointing. "To lead us to...that."

Landon laughed. This was crazy. He followed the point indicated and took off at a jog. There was one more Whump Tree to find, and he was definitely headed in the right "dreckshun."

"Come on!" Landon hollered. "Follow me, Melech! Echo echo green green!"

Chapter Fifteen

T he twentieth Whump Tree took Landon's breath away.
Unlike the others, it was an evergreen, with pine needles
as long as swords. Not only was it shaped like a colossal
Christmas tree (though Landon couldn't begin to see the
top of it), it also glowed like one. Dots of light illuminated
every bough rising up and up and up, creating an aura of
enchantment even in daylight. Landon couldn't get enough
of it. He was walking beneath its broad canopy like a child
catching snowflakes in his mouth. A whisper of air seemed to
flow up from his stomach, coming out his throat and mouth
in a continual "Ahhh. . ."

Landon was vaguely aware of Melech standing somewhat
uncomfortably nearby. How could he not be so enraptured by
the magnificent tree?

A voice came from high in the branches. "Ahoy! Ahoy! A

horse—and a boy!"

Landon stopped pacing, his neck feeling permanently
kinked. For a moment, he thought the tree itself was
speaking. "Hello, Mr. Tree!" he said, feeling deliriously giddy.
The tree seemed to revolve above him.

The dots of light gave away the movement of a branch.
The voice followed. "I see you; you can't see me! I see you;
you can't see me! You're way down there; I'm up a tree! Oh
fiddly-diddly-diddly-dee!"

But aren't you the tree? Landon wanted to say. Apparently
it wasn't. But the lively chattiness did bring to mind a squirrel.

Some needles began to fall. Landon remained so
transfixed that when one nearly parted his hair, he hardly
noticed. He did see the next needle that had turned and was
coming down sideways. Landon stepped back to avoid being
struck. That's when he noticed that the entire floor beneath
the tree was comprised of needles. The random crisscross
pattern gave it a woven mesh look. And what he had mistaken
for strangely shaped bushes—nearly as tall as himself—were
actually pinecones. Landon glanced quickly up. He did *not*
want one of those hitting him on the head.

A noise seemed to be coming from within the tree's great
trunk. Somehow it seemed oddly familiar. Landon stepped
closer to the rough bark, his heart beginning to pound. Could
those possibly be footsteps? Coming down? They stopped. A
few seconds later, he heard a soft, scratchy, ticking sound. He
imagined a squirrel (perhaps it really was a squirrel!) inside

with sharp claws tapping out Morse code.

Just before the tree opened, Landon remembered with a start and leaped back. He continued running backward, his eyes on the outwardly sliding segment of wood, until something hard and prickly took hold of him from behind.

"Hey!" he shouted. "Ow!"

But then he held his tongue. A figure was emerging from the tree, and it wasn't a squirrel.

"Hippity hop, it's time to stop, and time to say hello!"

A small, wiry man dressed in a dark green outfit with a matching top hat nimbly crossed the carpet of needles. He skidded to a stop and pressed two tiny fists against his hips, jutting his elbows like pointy wings. His sparkling blue eyes appeared to be laughing at Landon but not in a mocking sort of way. With a quick, insectlike movement, he thrust out a bony hand. "So let us shake, if you will take, my hand and up you go!"

Landon had barely brought up his right arm when he felt a clutch on his hand, and in one swift, shoulder-wrenching motion, his entire body was lifted from the ground. A brief glance over his shoulder revealed his spiny attacker—it was a pinecone.

The little man was sizing Landon up and down, his arms akimbo. Though his silver-buckled black shoes didn't move, he gave the impression he was skipping a circle around Landon as he surveyed him.

Feeling a bit awkward, Landon considered the man in

return. Tufts of orange hair crested his ears like feathery flames, and a matching thatch tipped his chin. His glistening eyes appeared as two animated blue marbles, dancing over an aquiline nose and teeth that, when he flashed a grin, were as straight and tight as a nutcracker's. The dark green coat and vest looked soft as velvet; each boasted several shiny silver buttons. White ruffles plumed like flowers from the V of his vest. A fine gold chain drooped from high inside the coat to a lower outside pocket.

Their eyes happened to meet, and for one hair-raising instant Landon had the uncanny feeling that he was looking into a mirror. In horror he realized he even had his hands on his hips—in fists—and he immediately dropped them. Despite this unsettling experience, Landon felt drawn to this seemingly ageless little man. He was a sprightly sprig of a fellow, quite fascinating to behold. And yes, they appeared nearly the same height, top hat excluded.

"What are you?" asked Landon, feeling extra curious. Before he could stop himself, the words spilled out. "A leprechaun?"

The man's eyes darkened, and he stomped his feet and pounded his legs with his fists. Then he stopped, clasped his hands together, and grinned, his eyes resuming their blue brilliance.

"Salutations and introductions, yes! Selfish *definitions*—oh no, no, no! Who's to say what I am or who you are? Maybe I'm a yam, and perhaps you are a star!" His orange eyebrows arched like two caterpillars rearing up at each other.

Landon felt baffled. Hadn't he just called him a boy from the tree? *Ahoy, ahoy, a horse—and a boy!* A horse. . . Where was Melech? Landon tried to sneak a glance around. He heard a jingling of chains and the snap of a whip followed by an agitated whinny.

"Melech!" Landon said, no longer concerned about his eccentric host. Over to his left near the bend of the trunk, two short figures in drooping caps and coveralls were trying to put a bridle and saddle on Melech. Somehow they had succeeded in lassoing a rope around his neck.

Landon started over. "Hey! Hands off him!"

Something grasped his arm like a talon and spun him around. A glint of dangling, swaying gold caught his eye and held it, back and forth, back and forth. The sounds of Melech's struggle faded. All Landon wanted was to watch this swinging gold fob forever.

A soothing voice dripped like syrup. "A mere formality and triviality, I'm afraid, of which you caught me on a technicality." A pair of blue eyes smiled at Landon from behind the pendulum. "And for that, me boy, please accept me most humblest and deepest apology."

Sadly Landon watched as the man pocketed the gold fob. The man quickly removed his hat and swept it to the ground. He bowed with such flourish, Landon felt a little self-conscious. This man with the fantastic gold fob was bowing to him, and beneath such an incredible tree!

Landon's face grew wondrously warm.

The man popped up and plopped on the hat. "Now, where were we? Oh, yes! Salutations and introductions, hello and here we go! Ludo is me name, and kudos is me game and me fame. It's all the same. And I am *very* glad you came!"

Ludo. Had Landon heard that name before? He couldn't place it. Everything seemed a bit fuzzy, as if his mind wasn't quite working properly. Landon wasn't too concerned, however, as long as he felt so deliciously warm and tingly.

"Oh," said Landon, remembering his manners. He could at least remember that much. "My name's Landon, and I am *very* glad to meet you, too!" He hoped he hadn't overdone things. It seemed important to make a good impression.

Ludo thrust out his orange-brushed chin and inserted one hand into his green coat like Napoleon. "Officially and diplomatically, it's Ludificor Stultus Avidus the Fourth. Supreme Reader of the Coin, crème de la crème, Leader of the Odds." Pulling his hand from his coat and putting it alongside his mouth, he added confidentially, "Between you and me and this here tree, I prefer plain old Ludo referentially to me."

Landon felt as if he'd just been given the secret to the universe. He hoped he looked trustworthy enough for this information. Not knowing what to say, he leaned close to Ludo and whispered back, "And I prefer Landon." His face immediately burned with embarrassment. What a foolish thing to say! Thankfully, his host seemed not to notice.

Ludo held up a twig-like finger. "As for the Odds, whom

I lead, well, what can I say? They're Odds!" He grinned and winked knowingly. Landon grinned stupidly back. "And as for the Coin, which I read"—his expression became much more serious, and Landon tried to match it—"well, you'll hear what I say when you witness the deed."

Commotion erupted nearby. Voices, chains, the whinnying of a horse. . .

Melech. What were they doing to—

A gold object flashed before Landon's eyes. Whatever he had become concerned over began to fade. He felt relieved, despite the claw-like grip on his shoulder.

"As I was saying, Landon. . ."

Between the swinging glimmers of gold were two blazing blue eyes, a pointy nose, straight teeth. . .

"There's no need to worry—don't worry—about the horse. We'll see that he receives proper care and treatment, of course, of course."

"But. . ." It was hard for Landon to speak, let alone concentrate. "But he's my friend. He saved my life—"

The gold pendulum became a whirring blur like a high-speed propeller. A voice seemed to float inside Landon's head. "Forget the horse. He's come and now he's gone. You have new friends here, who you are about to meet anon."

"New friends?" repeated Landon. He was happy to see his dear old friend Ludo grinning broadly at him. "I have new friends?" Landon could hardly contain his delight. Yet something was nagging at him. He couldn't quite place it.

"Out there you merely beat two Odds. But here you get to meet the Odds!"

"I beat two Odds?"

Ludo narrowed his eyes. "Not 'eowf,' Odd."

Landon remembered. There had been a creature—a short man—wearing blue coveralls and a droopy red cap. He had thought he might be a gnome, and then an elf. He was not an Awd, but an *Odd*. Of course! But how had Landon arrived at that first Whump Tree? (It was coming back to him in bits and pieces.) And how had he gone from there to here? Had he walked all that way through the forest? Or—

Ludo threw his hands in the air and arched his back like a gymnast. "Odds! Odds! Who are the Odds? The ones who toss the Coin and shout and cheer and clap applause!" Ludo brought his bony hands together and stamped his feet. "Huddle and muddle right here like a puddle! Trouble and bubble right now on the double!"

Branches shook overhead. Needles fell in a downpour, causing Landon to break into a frantic dance to avoid them. Bodies of little men—the Odds—were literally coming out of the woodwork. They streamed from the open tree, forming a ring around Landon and Ludo. The Odds laced their arms over each other's backs and leaned inward, slightly swaying. One final Odd wearing a pointed black cap joined the circle, and Ludo waved a signal toward the tree. As if by magic, the curved wooden door began to close. Its closing *whump* caused everyone to jump clear off the ground, returning to earth with a collective *thump*.

The needles had stopped falling. Landon was panting from his little jig and from the excitement of being suddenly surrounded by droopy- and pointed-cap-wearing Odds. Their constant swaying, accompanied by a low, moaning hum, was beginning to make him feel a little seasick.

Something fell with a thud from the tree as an afterthought to all the commotion. Landon assumed it was a pinecone and was glad he hadn't been standing beneath it. But pinecones don't bounce up and start walking, do they? The figure that approached—more in a stagger than a walk—appeared to be another Odd. Though there were others with yellow caps, his was the only cap to have not one point but three. With some jingles, he might have been a jester.

No one wanted to let this last Odd into the circle. He tried several places to no avail before Ludo gave an exasperated sigh and snapped his fingers. Immediately two Odds separated enough to let yellow three-points in, but they didn't look happy about it. When Ludo raised his hands, the swaying and murmuring ceased. Landon closed his eyes a moment as the rocking sensation subsided.

"You are here to meet our new guest." Ludo gestured toward Landon like he was a brand-new car on a game show. "His name is Landon, and he has passed the test!"

The Odds whooped and cheered uproariously. Landon didn't know where to look, going from grinning face to grinning face while trying not to smile too broadly or proudly himself. He glanced at the ground, wondering what all of the hullabaloo was about.

Ludo raised a finger, and the cheering stopped, though it continued echoing in Landon's ears. But it wasn't an echo. It was the sound of one Odd clapping in the forest. The Odd in the three-point hat clapped and stamped his feet and giggled in a gurgling, drooling sort of way. The other Odds shifted restlessly. Some of them openly sneered at him. Ludo snapped his fingers and brought down his hand like a spear. The giggling Odd stared at Ludo's finger with crossed eyes. His giggling stopped, and his grin slowly faded. A drop of saliva fell from the corner of his mouth, and then he was quiet. Landon felt a little sorry for him.

"Tardy Hardy," Ludo muttered, shaking his head. "Always late, even for a party."

Ludo raised his voice to address the group. "Our new friend here has a moniker. He calls himself Lan-*duhn*. But since he's passed the test, you shall call him Second-to-None!"

An excited murmur broke out. Landon heard his name and Second-to-None and the words *test, guest,* and *best* bantered about. It was like they were talking about him behind his back though he was standing in their midst. The nice thing was that everything they said was positive, and they truly seemed impressed. Of what had impressed them so much, Landon remained unsure. What test had he passed? What had he done, exactly? It hardly seemed to matter. He could go on soaking up this wonderful attention and admiration forever.

An Odd wearing a black cap spoke, breaking Landon's reverie. "We have some questions, if you please, to satisfy our curiosities."

"Oh," said Landon, wishing his mind wasn't so blank. "Okay."

"First, concerning Maple-Tree Max, our man on the perimeter."

The circle tightened as the Odds leaned in, their eyes boring into Landon like drills.

Black Cap stepped into the ring and paced around Landon, his hands clasped behind his back. At first, Landon began to pivot to keep facing him out of respect. But as the Odd kept circling, Landon finally stopped and glanced Black Cap's way when he passed in front of him.

The Odd paused and brought his hands to his mouth, pressing them together. He didn't look at Landon, which made Landon uneasy.

"Did Maple-Tree Max shoot more than, say, fifty arrows at you? Yes or no."

Landon swallowed. Fifty arrows? Ah. . .yes. The helicopter seeds. . .the maple tree. The creature with the arrows. It had been one of them! An Odd.

Landon swallowed. Oh, if only Holly were here. She would have known the answer. He kicked himself for not having counted the arrows. But how was he supposed to know there would be a test on it?

Wait a second. He was the guest who had *passed* the test,

Ludo had said. He was Second-to-None. Perhaps this wasn't a test about the actual number but about his character. How he would answer. It was fifty-fifty, yes or no. Landon took a deep breath. Everyone was watching him. Ludo had his twig-like arms crossed and was impatiently tapping a finger. One orange eyebrow was arched.

"Yes," Landon said. "Definitely more than fifty."

Everyone sighed, letting out their collectively held breath. Landon's black-capped questioner resumed pacing. He asked if Max had fired more than sixty arrows. Landon pretended to think on it but not for very long. "Yes," he responded, feigning confidence. "Yes, he did."

And so the questioning continued on up to ninety arrows. When Landon again answered in the affirmative, his inquirer removed his black cap and clutched it to his chest, kneading it nervously. Ludo waved him back into the circle, and Ludo himself stood before Landon.

Landon felt his heart begin to pound. His eyelids fluttered, and he felt moisture burst from beneath his armpits and dampen his palms. He tried to stop swallowing.

"Now, Second-to-None, no need to be nervous. You're among friends here."

Landon nodded weakly and rubbed his hands on his pants.

"Did Maple-Tree Max draw, aim, and release—to the best of your knowledge—at least ninety-one arrows in your general direction?"

Landon's throat had gone completely dry. When he tried

to speak, his voice cracked. He cleared his throat and tried again. "Yes," he said softly.

Ludo closed his eyes, absorbing this information. With his eyes still shut, he repeated the question, only this time asking if it had been at least ninety-*two* arrows. Landon nodded. Ninety-three? Ninety-four? Ninety-five? Yes, yes, yes. Ninety-six? Ninety-seven? Ninety-eight? Again Landon agreed with each number. Ludo opened his eyes and narrowed them. Landon felt as if his brain were being x-rayed. He tried to hide his doubts from Ludo's probing eyes.

Ludo took a half step nearer Landon. He flexed his bony finger in a hooking motion for Landon to lean toward him. Any closer now and Ludo's nose would be sticking in Landon's ear.

"One last question, Second-to-None. And you should be aware that this query is being monitored for verification, confirmation, and validation purposes. Are you ready?"

Landon thought he was going to faint.

"All right, then. In your esteemed estimation and to the best of your knowledge and cross your heart and hope to die, was there or was there not a ninety-ninth arrow launched by Max's sinuous bowstring?"

Cross his heart and hope to die? Landon didn't like the sound of that one bit. Though he hadn't seen any arrows or quivers or bows so far among these Odds, the thought of crossing his heart evoked a picture of a big *X* on his chest inviting any local archers to take their best shot. The world seemed to be waiting as Landon listened to Ludo wheezing through his nose.

Landon whispered, "Yes," and the wheezing stopped.

"Is that your conclusive response? Your definitive retort? Your final rejoinder?"

"Yes," Landon repeated.

Ludo stepped back and clapped his hands. "It's true, then, it's true! Ninety-nine times Maple-Tree Max fired and missed you. Ninety-nine shots, which means—you don't know what this means."

Landon shook his head. His knees felt wobbly, but he was still standing. And there was no black X on his chest for target practice.

"Maple-Tree Max is our Hundred-to-One Odd, boy. He's the Long Shot. If he missed you ninety-nine times, then woe to the next wayfarer who wanders into Ludo's Valley of the Odds!"

Ludo pressed both fists to his chest. He grimaced and staggered as if clutching at an arrow. It was too much. Landon felt his knees buckle, and down he went. The last thing he saw was Ludo's top hat falling and a shock of orange hair bursting forth like a candle flame.

Chapter Sixteen

A disturbing image came to Landon in the darkness. He saw a dark, four-legged creature being dragged off to a land of shadows. The creature was struggling and crying. No—it was neighing. It was a horse. A sharp pain stabbed Landon as a name came to mind but then faded again. Where were they taking this horse? What was going on?

He heard voices, except they didn't seem part of the vision. In fact, the voices seemed to drown out the vision. Landon tried to hold on, but soon he forgot it was a horse. And then the dark four-legged creature was gone. Meanwhile, the voices seemed to grow stronger, and they sounded very close by. Though Landon could understand most of the words, he had no idea what they were actually talking about.

"He's a tough one, Master Ludificor. Snapped three ropes

already. Strongest and strangest aminal we've seen in years."

"Because he's the only animal you've seen in years, you dimwit. And those ropes have rotted. Go bind a fresh tether and take him to Wagglewhip."

"But Master, a fresh tether? We haven't done that in years. . .not sure anyone remembers."

"I want it before the Coin rises. You have until then."

"Master Ludificor, the resources. . .our skills. . .lost to—"

"Do it now, Trumplestump. *Now*. You'll lose more than your skills and resources if it's not done before—"

The voices stopped abruptly. Landon heard some shuffling or scuffling about. Then someone whispered, "Hush! The boy's stirring."

The next voice rang clear and shrill in Landon's ear.

"Second-to-None! Lan-*duhn*! Boy! *Up* you go!"

Something was pulling at his arms and pushing at his back. Landon was sitting, and then he was falling back again except something caught him and hoisted him up. His entire body was off the ground. He was floating.

Landon opened his eyes. Stars twinkled overhead. As they came into focus, however, they weren't stars but little lights at various heights among long dark needles and thick branches. He was bouncing gently along beneath a glorious tree. Wait. He remembered. It was the Whump Tree. But how—

"He's awakened!" cried a familiar voice. And then a chorus of voices broke into song:

A jolly good fellow is he-ee!
We found him under our tree-ee!
He outran the arrows of Max—all ninety-nine!
He told us himself how he stacks—Second-to-None!
So to the green we must take him to see-ee. . .
The Coin that we toss every day-ay!
Whenever we hear Ludo say-ay!
"Heave!" (Ho, Ludo!)
"Heave!" (Ho, Ludo!)
When the sun comes and when the sun goes away-ay. . . .

Landon wasn't floating. He was resting on a bed of stubby hands atop the arms of several Odds. They had carried him to the edge of the tree's canopy and stopped, their fingers twitching with seeming restlessness. One particularly wriggly hand was gripping the area behind Landon's right knee, tickling it tremendously. Tears formed at the corners of Landon's eyes as he tried desperately to control himself. But he couldn't take it. He burst out laughing, and the Odds beneath him scattered like startled sheep.

Landon fell and braced himself for impact. But the ground never came. He was resting in two sturdy arms about three feet up. He turned to face the huge, gap-toothed grin of an Odd wearing a yellow cap with three drooping points. Tardy Hardy, Landon remembered. The Odd let out a single snorting giggle and set Landon gently down.

"Thanks," said Landon. Something about Tardy Hardy's

eyes made Landon look into them longer than he normally would have. He saw something there—behind the eyes—that made him think this Odd wasn't as dopey as he seemed. When Tardy Hardy suddenly winked, Landon jumped back, startled.

A bony hand grasped Landon's shoulder. "Ha-ha!"

Landon turned. "Ludo," he said, blinking. Something about the skinny, green-clad man in a top hat made Landon want to shrink back in fear, though he wasn't sure why.

Ludo's blue eyes flashed, and Landon realized there was a bank of bright sunlight to his right. The edge of the tree's canopy skirted what appeared to be a huge, open field. Landon blinked again. The grass was gorgeously green and short like the turf on a golf course. The vast clearing appeared round, like a giant circle.

"Me most humblest apologies again, Landon, Second-to-None." He bowed and then came up, but something about this didn't seem quite right. "These Odds are not accustomed to such a dignitary as yourself. Please forgive us our lack of preparedness and general clumsiness and downright awkwardness." Ludo giggled strangely. "And please, please, *please* disregard Tardy Hardy there altogether."

Where had he gone? Landon glanced back under the tree, where everything seemed dark after staring at the sun-drenched field. At first he couldn't find him. Then his gaze drifted back to a giant pinecone that had three yellow, droopy prongs protruding from behind it. It looked like a dark, overripe pineapple.

Ludo's knuckles dug into Landon's back, directing him toward the clearing. "And now, me boy, let me show you our true pride and joy. The site of the valley's most beautiful scene, I present to you, the Echoing Green."

Ludo removed his top hat and bowed deeply, extending one arm to the side. His orange hair flopped over until Ludo popped up again, putting his hat back on. He crossed his arms, glancing this way and that. Finally he turned to shout over his shoulder. "I said, 'The site of the valley's most beautiful scene. . .the Echoing Green'!"

The Odds, who had apparently gone into hiding after Landon had burst out laughing, now came running to the fore. As they scampered onto the clearing, Ludo pointed to each one in turn as if picking them off with a pistol. "There's Half-the-Time Harvey, also known as Fifty-Fifty. That's Three-to-One Thurman. There's Six-to-One Slim, who could stand to lose some weight, quite frankly. There's Five-to-Two Frank, by the way, who we like to call Double Prime."

The Odds could run surprisingly fast. It was a long way across the field, yet all but Six-to-One Slim had made it to the other side and disappeared among the trees. They had all run to different places, however, fanning out at equal distances. It had been a fascinating event to watch.

Ludo had taken out a gold fob and was tapping it as if getting impatient. When he noticed Landon looking at the fob, he slipped it back inside his jacket.

"Many of the other Odds are Ten-to-One or older, so you

see what poor Ludificor must put up with." Ludo nudged Landon in the ribs as if he'd just shared an inside joke.

"None of them look very old or young to me," said Landon. "Especially you, Ludo."

Ludo frowned but quickly replaced it with a smile. He giggled curiously, and the sound made Landon clench his teeth and cringe. "Old! Of course they're not old, they're Odds! But," he lowered his voice to a whisper, "some Odds are greater than others. And they'd better work this time." He stepped away from Landon and into the sunlight. Raising his hands to the sky, he said, "The Echoing Green!"

Three voices came back from various points across the field.

"The bludgeoning spleen!"

"A troublesome tween!"

"I know what you mean!"

Twisting around with a beatific smile plastered on his face, Ludo clapped his hands. "And that," he said, "is that. Which leads us, of course, to this. Follow me and come and see." Landon hesitated, and Ludo laughed. "Come, come, me boy! Ahoy, ahoy. We've a magnificent toy we're about to deploy!" He leaned back and laughed, his teeth opening and then snapping like a nutcracker's. With that, he turned and skipped into the field.

Landon stepped warily onto the grass. It was like walking on carpet. Even through the soles of his boots, he could feel the luxurious plushness. Seeing Ludo skip ahead of him like a little kid made Landon want to laugh and skip as well. So he did. What fun! It was like playing at the park. The sun was on its way down toward the treetops at the far end of the Echoing Green. As Landon neared the center, where Ludo awaited him, he could tell the clearing was perfectly round. He was in the middle of a big green circle.

Ludo was studying his gold fob. As Landon skipped cheerfully toward him, he thought Ludo must be looking at a pocket watch, or perhaps a compass, the way it held his attention. But when he drew near and snuck a quick peek, he saw there were no numbers or hands. It was simply a gold disk attached to a delicate string of tiny gold links. Ludo tilted it back and forth so that it reflected glimmers of sunlight. Ludo seemed to give a start when he noticed Landon standing next to him. He covered the fob and deposited it inside his jacket.

A very strange feeling came over Landon, sort of like déjà vu—he had been here before. But somehow he knew that that wasn't true. It was impossible. Was it a dream he was remembering? He could see himself on a cliff overlooking a valley. It was getting dark. Something suddenly flashed—a tiny gold light—down in the valley. It had appeared to come from the center of a circle. And there were cheers, or voices crying, "Ohhh-whoa."

Landon shook his head. He hadn't heard those voices, had he? It seemed there had been someone else there with him. Another person had heard the voices and told him about them. *A thousand voices. . .*

But who was that person? For the life of him, Landon

couldn't remember. It was as if part of his memory had been erased. And wherever this other person was—*he'd been a good friend,* Landon remembered sadly, *a true companion*—there remained only a featureless ghost or phantom. No, not even that much. All that was left was a faint, lingering shadow.

Two glaring blue eyes startled Landon back to the green. "Hello, Second-to-None, hello! We're about to get ready for the big show. You may remain here, but off Ludificor must soon go."

"But you just invited me out here," said Landon. "What's the 'big show' all about?"

"The time has come for a flip of the wrist and a flick of the thumb! Will it rise? Will it set? Oh, the fun has just begun!"

"What time?" said Landon. "What time is it, anyway?"

Ludo shrugged, and his eyes appeared to darken. "No time to explain, Second-to-One. We must gather the Odds for the Great Observance."

Landon could feel his heart rate quicken. "What Observance?"

"For me reading of the Coin, me lad. Me reading of the Coin."

Ludo flung wide his arms and swiveled about like the master of ceremonies standing center-ring at the circus. "Festoon the Doubloon!"

"Release the balloon!" came a voice from the left.

"Don't spit on a baboon!" shouted a voice from the right.

"Man the spoon! Man the spoon!" called a voice from directly ahead.

Ludo spun back around and placed one hand on each of Landon's shoulders, where they clutched and kneaded like talons. Landon winced and began to feel a little faint. *Not again,* he thought, resisting as tears formed at the corners of his eyes. He tried to stand firm, but when Ludo released one shoulder to prop two bony fingers beneath Landon's chin, he couldn't help but meet Ludo's mesmerizing gaze.

"I'm the fourth generation Reader of the Coin, me lad. The great gold Coin that marks our days."

Landon squirmed, and Ludo's grip only tightened. "How do you read a coin?" Landon asked, thinking of the gold disk Ludo seemed so fond of. "I mean, what do you read on it? What does it say?"

Ludo's gaze drifted off, and his clasp slightly loosened. Landon let his shoulder sag, and he breathed deeply. When Ludo looked again at Landon, his eyes were still a little cloudy. "How do you like your eggs, Second-to-None?"

Landon looked at him, wondering if this was a joke. "My eggs?" he asked.

Ludo frowned. "You've had eggs, have you not? How do you like them cooked? On a stove or in a pot?"

"Uh, fried, I guess—no, wait. Scrambled. I like scrambled eggs." His stomach growled for emphasis.

"Ah, me." Ludo shook his head. He let go of Landon's shoulder, and his hand seemed to crawl with a mind of its own toward his dark green coat. It emerged from behind the velvety lapel fingering the gold disk. "Me, me, me." Ludo continued to shake his head, seemingly not aware of the fob resting in his palm. "Let me see, see, see. What about *sunny side up*, me friend? For that is what I read on the Coin. It tells me when the sun is up"—he lifted the gold fob high—"and when the sun is down"—he lowered his hand.

Landon glanced over Ludo's hat at the sun, which was beginning to brush the treetops. Landon squinted and lowered his eyes. "Why don't you just look at it—the sun? What do you need a coin for?"

Ludo's nostrils flared. "Me boy, no one questions the Coin. And since I am the Reader of it, no one questions *me,* either."

A creaking, grinding, rumbling noise came from the side of the field. The ground began to tremble. A company of Odds marched out from the trees, pulling ropes that went up at an angle after them. They were towing something big. Two large wooden wheels appeared, and then a contraption on top of the cart came into view. It looked something like a giant wooden spoon raised between massive logs. The ropes were lashed to the handle, and something thick and gold was resting on the spoon.

Ludo slowly backed up as the Odds lugged the spoon out onto the lawn. He started to speak, but it almost seemed he was talking to himself. "How do I read the Coin, you ask? How does Ludificor Stultus Avidus the Fourth *read* such a gorgeous gargantuan Coin?" He giggled in a high voice, which Landon could barely hear over the heavy rumble.

As the ground shuddered more violently, Landon felt his eyes grow wide and his jaw fall open. That was the Coin they were pulling in? Yes, the gold object atop the giant spoon was the Coin.

Landon walked backward as the Odds drew the cart to the middle of the Echoing Green. He gaped up at the beams, the ropes, the enormous spoon. . .and the glinting gold. With a shout, the Odds stood up and the ropes went slack.

Landon saw Ludo out of the corner of his eye. As they stood together, side by side, admiring the structure before them, Landon felt his animosity toward Ludo slip away. He was glad he had been invited onto the green for this event. Even the clutching pain in his shoulder began to ebb.

The whole sun-up and sun-down thing still didn't make sense. But Landon wondered how Ludo could even see the Coin, let alone read it, whatever that meant. "How do you read the Coin, Ludo?" he asked.

Ludo spoke in a faraway voice. "Up in me tree, laddie, up in me tree. Where I have me lenses and only I can see, only I can see. So when the Coin is tossed thricely, they all listen to me, they all listen to me."

"But how—"

Ludo took hold of Landon's arm, though he didn't pinch it or squeeze. "No more questions, me boy, no more questions. Do we agree?"

"Well, it is beautiful," Landon said. "But I still don't

understand why you need to read—"

"Augh!" Ludo took off his hat and threw it to the ground. He jumped on it repeatedly, his orange shock of hair flicking like the flame on a lighter. "I said *no more questions*, agree?"

Landon watched in detached amazement. "I was only wondering what the reason was."

Ludo leaped over and stabbed the air in front of Landon's face. "And Ludo's beginning to wonder why ye are beginning to sound like Vates, a despicable old man whom I hates." Ludo pronounced the last word like Hades, which rhymed with the earlier word, "Vay-tees."

The sound of the strange name and seeing the fire of hatred within Ludo caused something to burn inside Landon as well. "Vates," he said, testing the sound of it on his tongue. "Who is Vates?"

Ludo just about did a back flip. He jumped on his hat until it was flatter than the grass around it. "Augh! Augh! Augh! AUGH! Vates's always asking questions and warning and wondering. Crazy old coot! There's no use in thinking any more than stinking. All is chance. It revolves around the toss of the Coin—our Coin! The Odds gather for Sun Up and Sun Down. We are safe here in our little lucky town. Safe from the daft queries of Vaticinator."

Ludo's face shone red and his eyes glowered like thunderclouds. He panted like a mad beast.

Landon's heart hammered and his mind hummed. "Did you say 'All is chance'?"

Ludo seemed not to hear him. He spat and raised a knotted fist. "Vates' name I despise, and all he implies. It's just lies, lies, lies, *lies*." With surprising swiftness, he kicked the dilapidated hat high into the air. It soared like a clay pigeon and then fell to the ground. "All is chance, Lan-*duhn*. All is chance."

Words began to flood Landon's head:

> *Could it be chance, mere circumstance*
> *That man eats cow eats grass eats soil*
> *And then man dies, and when he lies*
> *To soil he does return?*

The sky's color was draining. The shadow of the giant spoon stretched across Landon in the direction of the towering pine, the Whump Tree. Ludo started in that direction as well, but then he paused and spoke to Landon over his shoulder. "Now you've wasted too much of me precious time, boy. Enough is enough. When I do me reading of the Coin, ye had best be seen and not heard. 'Tis not wise to meddle with chance nor interfere with circumstance."

Landon couldn't believe what he was hearing. *Chance* and *circumstance*, the very same words! Before Ludo reached the edge of the green, Landon called after him. "Where is Vates now?"

Ludo arched his back and screamed as if he'd been shot from behind. Then he disappeared beneath the tree.

From the other side of the field came the late echo. "Who took the lady's cow?"

Chapter Seventeen

T he Odds who had hauled out the spoon and the
Coin remained quietly among the dangling ropes.
Meanwhile, shadowy figures filled the spaces beneath the
trees around the Echoing Green. They were gathering for
the reading of the Coin.

For some reason, Landon picked up Ludo's flat hat.
Landon used to like to have a reason for everything, but so
many absurd and fantastic things had happened to him that
he simply hadn't the time to figure everything out. Maybe
someday that's what he would do, figure everything out. For
now, it was time to get off the green. Landon had a feeling
something was about to happen. He could sense the energy
and anticipation in the air.

As he walked across the carpetlike grass, his mind reeled
with thoughts of the Coin and the mysterious Vates and Ludo

and chance. He punched out the top of the hat from the inside and thought about putting it on. But then he decided he'd better not. He stuck out like a sore thumb enough without having to worry about Odds mistaking him for Ludo. Wishing he'd left the hat where it was, Landon simply held on to it as he stepped in among the throng.

The Odds parted, glancing and staring. Landon was glad it was beginning to get dark so they couldn't see his face, which he knew from its warmth was quite red. He was surprised to see female Odds and tiny children Odds. Since they hadn't been around earlier, he hadn't considered their existence a possibility. One tiny one tugged at her mother's hand and pointed. Landon smiled, and she let out a whimper.

Relieved to finally find himself in the back of the crowd, Landon looked out at the green. In the deepening dusk he realized that the Whump Tree lights were dimming as well. That seemed strange, that they'd be on in the daytime and off at night. A faint hazy aura about the towering tree was all that remained.

Landon felt a tinge of loneliness creeping up, standing among so many strangers. He again tried to think of that someone whom he couldn't think of. A friend and companion who was but a nameless, faceless shadow. Landon felt sad. Whoever it was, he missed him.

A hush descended. Landon held his breath. From high in the Whump Tree, a shrill voice pierced the air. Landon had a good idea whose it was.

"Heave!" cried the voice.

The thunderous response caused chills to run up Landon's spine. "Ho, Ludo!"

Something happened out in the field. The Odds beneath the spoon had yanked their ropes downward, plunging the handle toward the ground and sending the spoon end into the air. As the giant lever reached its limit, the carriage shuddered and the Coin was launched. It was the most astounding sight Landon had ever seen.

Rising above the treetops, the golden Coin seemed to defy gravity. It threw back an array of colors and light, reflected from the unseen sun. Finally it began its descent. The rope-handlers had scattered safely away, except for one. Landon gasped as the Coin struck the spoon, plummeting toward the carriage while the handle flew up. The one Odd had simply been staring, apparently unable to let go of his rope. He rose instantly, and when his head collided with the wood, an audible crack was heard. The crowd cringed and oohed as the unfortunate Odd fell limply with a soft thud.

Three figures came running from the tree line. One of them stumbled and rolled and popped right up again, hardly breaking his stride. Two of them took hold of the fallen rope-handler's armpits and began to drag him away. The third—the one who had stumbled—grabbed the swinging rope, which had come back down with the lever. The other rope-pullers returned to their ropes as well.

It all happened so fast, Landon had the eerie feeling it

wasn't the first time such an accident had occurred. Of course it wasn't a complete accident, which meant that no one was responsible or to blame. The poor rope-puller could only blame himself for not letting go.

Ludo's voice rang out from the tree. "Heave!"

"Ho, Ludo!"

Landon reacted in time to join in on "Ludo!" It felt good being part of the crowd. The Coin went up, flipping and flashing in the sky. Suddenly it all came together. This is what Landon had seen from the cliff, the glimmering Coin! And the "thousand voices" were the Odds rimming the Echoing Green. What was it they had said? "Ohhh-whoa"? That was "Ho, Ludo"! Landon felt a smile form on his face. He had figured it out! He wanted to share this with someone, with that phantom friend, the forgotten shadow. But of course his friend wasn't there, and Landon's smile faded with sadness.

The Coin landed without incident, sending up the ropes like electrified spider legs. When they came swinging back down, the rope-pullers stepped back in, held them taut, and waited.

One final time Ludo issued his command, and again the Odds and Landon chanted in reply: "Ho, Ludo!"

Like a band of cathedral bell ringers, the Odds lunged simultaneously. The Coin flew straight up, flashed its brilliance, and returned heavily to the spoon. It was better than fireworks.

Landon was feeling peacefully numb. He felt neither tired

nor awake, hungry nor full, happy nor sad. He was beginning to feel like one of them. That is, like an *Odd*. Except that it didn't feel odd at all. It felt normal, somehow. And Landon thought he was fine.

The spoon and the rope-pullers and the Coin seemed to be dissolving into darkness. Already Landon was eager to see the Coin again. But if it was only tossed twice a day, well, that's the way it was.

A few stars twinkled. Landon failed to appreciate the beauty of the night, however. What were a few stars compared to the dazzling display of the Coin? After beholding its radiance, nothing could be nearly so spectacular. It seemed everything in life would now be fairly dull. . .except for the Coin. Just like that, it had become the only thing that mattered.

Ludo's voice dispelled the quiet. "I have read the Coin."

"Ho, Ludo. He's read the Coin!" people murmured.

"The great Coin has revealed to me, Ludificor Stultus Avidus the Fourth, another day has ended in our valley. And so here by the Echoing Green, I do so solemnly and sanctimoniously declare, that after much careful observance and considerable contemplation, it is Sun Down!"

"Sun Down!" Their cheer resounded. "Ho, Ludo!"

Landon patted the backs of the people standing in front of him, and they turned and shook his hand, as if welcoming him to a secret club. Landon continued to exchange grips and say "Ho, Ludo" both as a greeting and a farewell. The Odds nodded to him politely; even the tiny ones no longer seemed alarmed.

It was nice to be accepted, yet as he watched them departing for their trees or wherever they had come from, Landon felt an aching hollowness. But there was hope. For he knew that tomorrow he would get to see the great Coin rising again into the sky. And when he cheered, "Ho, Ludo!" once more with the crowd, everything would be all right.

A creaky, rumbling noise was fading across the field. Landon ran out under the stars and looked around. The Echoing Green was deserted, the spoon and Coin already towed away. The silence was almost maddening. No crickets, no frogs, no owls, nothing. Landon whispered again and again to himself and imagined the din of a thousand voices joining in: *Ho, Ludo! Ho, Ludo! Ho, Ludo!* He was still holding his leader's hat, and he put it on proudly. Then he skipped across the field toward the trees through which he thought they had hauled the Coin. He was thinking of inquiring about joining the rope-pullers' brigade.

Landon couldn't find the Coin or anyone to talk to about it. He wandered among the trees as if in a dream, talking nonsense to himself and twirling a pretend gold fob on a chain. Every now and then he would pause, tilt his head, remove Ludo's top hat, and bow with a flourish, sweeping the hat around and then in to his chest. He was in this position with his face to the ground when he heard what sounded like two firecrackers popping close by. *Bang-bang!*

Landon performed a startled jumping jack and inadvertently threw the hat into a bush. As he was reaching for it, two more bursts sounded—*pop-pop*! Landon flinched and then froze. What on earth was going on? His fingertips were touching the hat, but he moved no farther, instead trying to see a possible source for the noise. Nothing but trees and bushes and, through a small break overhead, a ragged patch of sky was in view.

Landon sighed. "Ho, Ludo," he muttered and grabbed the hat.

Clap-clap!

"Augh!" Landon waved the hat before him as if he'd encountered an invisible web. "Get away from me, whatever you are!" he said. "Leave me alone."

A thin hand appeared before him. *Snap-snap!* The fingers flickered, and then the hand was gone.

Landon flailed his arms again vigorously. "Stop that! What are you doing to me?"

A light, high voice giggled, and the bush appeared to wiggle. Was it a fairy of some sort? he wondered. It sounded like a girl. Landon leaned warily close to the bush. "Who's there?" he whispered. "What are you?"

A figure hopped out like lightning. *Tap-tap!* Landon was struck twice on the nose and went reeling backward, thrashing the air around his head. "I said *stop that*. Augh!" He bumped against a tree and stood, nervously looking about. He blinked uncontrollably as if he'd been temporarily blinded from a flashbulb. Landon tried to steady his breathing.

"What do you want with me?" He didn't know where to direct his voice.

Something was waving before his eyes in a blur. It slowed down until Landon could see it was a hand. The thin hand from before. He braced himself, expecting a slap or a snap or a tap, but the hand noiselessly withdrew. In front of the bush stood a girl who appeared about his own age. "Can you see me now?" she asked softly, a corner of her mouth raised in a smirk.

"Of course I see you," said Landon. "You're right there."

The other corner of her mouth rose to form a smile. "Well, you weren't seeing me a minute ago."

Landon frowned, wondering what sort of game she might be playing. "You were moving too fast," he said testily. "You were like a blur."

She giggled, and the sound of it made Landon think of bubbles breaking away from soapy foam. "You were moving too slow," she said teasingly. "I was just like I am now."

Landon looked at her in disbelief. "No way." He shook his head. Even as he said it, however, he began to wonder.

"I did hide behind the bush," she admitted. "Otherwise all I did was this." She clapped her hands, and Landon flinched, although it wasn't loud or startling. "And this." She snapped her fingers, and the sound was like the rubbing of two dry leaves. "Oh, and I did touch your nose."

"I thought you were throwing firecrackers at me," Landon said. His face was suddenly growing warm, and he had to look at the ground. He could tell she was still smiling at him.

"No throwing," she said, "except for you throwing that hat. And anyway, I don't know how to crack fire."

Landon shook his head. "I don't understand. What happened to me? I mean, all of a sudden I feel totally different. Like I had just been—"

"In a trance," she said. And Landon slowly lifted his gaze and nodded. "You were," she said, "and I'm just glad I got to you in time. One more glimpse of the Coin and you might have been under its spell forever."

The girl extended her hand to Landon. "Come on," she said. "We need to hurry. I want to show you some things, and then, well, come on."

Landon held out the top hat, and the girl cringed as if it were a dead rabbit. He tossed it aside and grabbed her hand. "Where are we going?" he asked.

"To the tree," she said, and somehow Landon knew which one she meant.

"What do you want to show me there?" At the touch of her hand, Landon's heart started to pound. He was grateful the darkness concealed his blushing face.

"Some signs," she said, pulling him along through the trees. "They think they're from Vates. And I think he left them for you."

Chapter Eighteen

The Echoing Green came into view as a dull, treeless void, but the girl didn't enter it. She led Landon around the perimeter, staying just within the tree line. Her hand felt at once delicate and strong, light and lively. The very touch of it seemed to give Landon renewed strength.

As quickly and nimbly as the girl moved through the trees—she obviously knew her way even in the dark—Landon was able to keep up with no problem. At one point he wondered if he might be floating after her as a kite rather than running on his own power.

They reached the massive trunk of the Whump Tree. All the little lights were out. When the girl slipped her hand from Landon's grasp, he sighed. His face felt warm, and he was breathing rapidly, but he attributed these symptoms to the run, not to the girl.

"We're just in time," she said. "Look."

Landon gasped and wanted to run. Two Odds were marching right toward them! The girl remained calm and steady, however, so Landon held his ground. The Odds, it turned out, were marching toward the door of the tree, one stepping several feet behind the other. The door was farther round the trunk, and as long as Landon and the girl didn't move, they probably wouldn't be spotted. Landon held his breath.

The reason one Odd followed the other was because they were carrying something between them. "They found another sign," the girl whispered excitedly. "Vates must have been here."

The sign she referred to looked like a rolled-up carpet. A rope or two trailed from either end.

"My uncle sends out a search team every night after he reads the Coin." She glanced at Landon. "If they find a sign, they tear it down. And if they find—"

"Your uncle reads the Coin?" Landon asked, stunned. "He's. . .Ludo?"

She nodded and then held up her hand for silence.

The Odds had stopped about ten feet from the trunk. The leader seemed to be peering up at the tree and speaking in a hushed voice. "Addlefoot! Open up, we're here! We found one!"

A voice hissed back. "Passwords please?"

"Get off it, Addlefoot! It's us. We've got a sign, for Ludo's sake! Open the door!"

"Passwords please!"

"*Nutmeg* and *ratchet,* you fidgetbottom. Now open— "

The tree began to vibrate ever so slightly, almost like a hum. Something was moving inside it, and Landon could hear a series of clicks. Though he was well away from the door, he braced himself for what was coming.

Rrrrhhuup! A large piece of the trunk swung outward, spilling light into the forest. The Odds marched inside, muttering under their breaths. No sooner had they slipped from view than the girl grabbed Landon's hand and yanked him forward, saying, "Come on!"

They skirted the tree and stepped right inside, into the amber light. Landon squinted and shielded his eyes. But the girl said, "Cover your ears." He hesitated less than a second before closing his eyes and pressing his hands to his ears. A half second later, the earth shuddered and the tree closed with a *boom* that resounded like the inside of a big bass drum.

Several seconds later, Landon felt a gentle tapping on his arm. "It's okay now. You can open your eyes and ears."

Several lanterns illuminated the space. Some lanterns hung from crossbeams, while others sat on tables or benches. As Landon's eyes adjusted, he could see the room stretched farther back, though it was only lit near the entrance. On the floor before him lay a pile of carpetlike rolls, though he could see that they were made of thick, fibrous material like burlap. Landon looked at his pants. They were darker, but the texture appeared quite similar. The top roll, he presumed, was the one the Odds had just brought in and added to the heap.

Stacked along the wall to the right were picket signs of various sizes. A staircase led up. Beyond the immediate circle of light, Landon could make out more rugged tables and benches. In the far left corner appeared a long counter, like a bar. Behind it rose a bank of shelves filled with bottles, and a glass-fronted cabinet with crisscrossing slats. The cabinet doors and bottles were frosted with dust. Cobwebs draped between the shelves and two goblets on the bar. The room looked like a long-forgotten saloon in a ghost town. Except now it was used for storing signs found out in the woods.

"Where did they go?" Landon whispered, meaning the two Odds.

The girl pointed to the staircase. "They always drop the sign and run. Can't handle the boom." She raised all her fingers and widened her eyes. Then she smiled.

Landon felt his lips twitching upward, but he thought he should appear serious, especially now that they could see each other plainly in the light. The girl's eyes were big even before she widened them. Her hair was fairly long with a crinkly wave running through it.

"You said Vates left the signs?"

The girl quickly nodded, then gestured with her head for him to follow. She went to the pile of rolled canvases and kicked the top one open. It unrolled over the pile and onto the floor. As the words inside were revealed, Landon felt the air being sucked right out of his lungs.

Beware the one who seems not young or old
He will betray your trust
You have been foretold

Beware the lure of shimmering gold
That turns the mind to rust
And the heart to mold

Beware, my friends, do not be misled
The Odds are against you
They may want you dead

"Why?" Landon started. "Why do you think this was written for me?"

The girl's eyes narrowed as she studied Landon's face. "Can you read?" she asked.

Landon looked at her. "Of course I can read."

"That's why," she said. "No one here can except for my uncle. Which is why I wondered why he always wanted the signs taken down, unless they were meant for someone else." She leaned closer. "Someone else who was coming to read them."

Landon was beginning to feel a little dizzy. "You can't read?" he asked.

She sadly shook her head. "Words lost their meaning here when. . .come look at these other signs." She took Landon's hand and led him to the wall against which were leaning dozens of wooden boards on pickets. "What does this one say?"

She flipped one around—they were all facing the wall—and Landon felt even more faint as he read the top line. He closed his eyes a moment and tried to get his bearings. Opening his eyes, he began to read:

> *Could it be chance, coincidence?*
> *That sun turns earth turns moon turns seas*
> *And so there are years, and salty beach tears*
> *So ticks celestial time.*

A line above the poem read, "The Auctor's Riddle Part II."

Landon pressed his fingers to his temples and rubbed. Then he flipped through more of the signs. They were all the same: part two of the Auctor's Riddle. He ran back to the pile of rolled canvases and opened the next one and then another. They all carried the same message of warnings about one who seemed neither young nor old *(Ludo,* Landon thought with a chill), about the lure of shimmering gold (*the Coin*), and about the Odds—who may want him. . .*dead*?

Landon looked suspiciously at the girl, who was standing looking down at him with no readable expression on her face. He swallowed. "Is there a way to get out of here? I think I'd better be going."

He glanced around, searching for an exit. The curved wall of wood appeared solid in each direction, however. High overhead in the shadows arched what appeared to be a ceiling of twisted roots. Landon was beginning to feel claustrophobic. Had he been lured into a trap?

"What's wrong?" she said. "You seem nervous." She reached down to touch him.

Landon cringed, watching her hand come toward his shoulder as if it were a snake. But deep down he wanted to trust her. He thought he could trust her—she had woken him from the spell of the Coin, hadn't she?

"It's the sign," said Landon, panting. "It says. . .it says the Odds might want to kill me."

The girl drew back in horror. "What? Why would Vates write that?"

Landon read through the three warnings aloud, checking her expression as she heard the words for the first time. The girl's mouth hung open, and a tiny tear dripped from the corner of one eye. Finally, she sighed. "Not *dead*, dead," she explained. "They only want you dead in here"—she clutched at the middle of her chest—"to turn your heart to rust and your mind to mold, like the rest of them."

Landon stood and wanted to touch her shoulder, but he refrained. "Why are you different?" he said. "How come you're not entranced and, well, *dead*."

She smiled tenderly and looked sad as could be. "Because when the Coin goes up, I close my eyes, and I try to remember. . . ."

Her eyes shut and another tear fell down her cheek. Her voice dropped to a hollow whisper.

"I try to remember the time. . .before the Shadows came."

The back of Landon's neck tingled. He could have sworn all the shadows in the place had shifted, though none of the lights had moved or even flickered.

The girl opened her eyes. "I really shouldn't talk about it, not here. But things were different. This place was alive with nightly feasts." She waved her hand, indicating the empty, dusty tables and benches. "The Odds were creative craft-folk, full of music and poetry and laughter. And the forest—oh, the forest!" Her gaze lifted toward the ceiling, though she seemed to be seeing things from the past. "It was full of life and the songs of the animals."

A voice came from the stairway, and Landon froze. The tone was terribly familiar.

"Who is that I hear inside my tree? Could that be my niece, my little Ditty? Come up to visit your dear Uncle Ludo, my sweet pretty!"

The girl looked at Landon. "My name's Ditty," she said. "We better go."

Landon wanted to nod, but he couldn't even do that, his body was so petrified. He watched in amazement as the girl—Ditty—reached into a lantern and plucked the flame right out of it. The light continued to glow between her thumb and forefinger, seemingly floating there. She held it before his eyes, and Landon was just as surprised to see it wasn't a flame but an insect. It was a lifeless firefly, lifeless except for its steady glow, that is. It was actually hovering inside a clear bubble.

Ditty lifted Landon's hand and set the bubble in it.

"We might need this," she said. "Hide it until we get out of range."

The bubble was virtually weightless but hard as plastic. Landon managed to close his fingers around it.

"It's just me, Uncle Ludo!" Ditty hollered toward the stairs. "But I'm leaving now!"

"Oh, for why, sweetie pie?" The shrill voice made Landon's skin crawl.

Ditty took hold of Landon's shoulders and gently shook him. "We have to go, now." A funny look came over her face. "I have a surprise for you, you know. Come on."

A surprise? Landon almost laughed. He'd had more surprises lately than he'd imagined he could have in a lifetime. He took a deep breath and mustered his strength, and Ditty helped by lifting his elbow. Landon tucked the neat firefly ball inside the top of his boot, and Ditty drew him to the wall near the entryway. She lifted a wooden flap that Landon never would have found and put her mouth to the opening. "Addlefoot!" she said in a strange, hoarse voice.

"Ah? Eh? A-*hem*. Sir Ludo? Is that you? Addlefoot Treeberry, at your service!"

Ditty whispered to Landon. "Say 'nutmeg and ratchet.' My voice hurts. Please?"

A series of creaking noises came from the stairway. It sounded like someone was coming down.

Landon leaned close to the hole. He tightened his throat.

"Nutmeg and ratchet!" His voice cracked halfway through, ending on a squeak. He waited anxiously, hoping he wouldn't have to say anything else into the hole.

A scratching noise seemed to come from the wood. Landon tilted his head. Somewhere above them, a series of clicks sounded. *Tick, tick, tick, tick.* The room gave a shudder, and the wall opened, swinging outward.

In the hazy light outside the tree, Landon paused and then nearly staggered at the sight before him. There was Tardy Hardy, grinning from one droopy yellow point of his hat to another. He was holding a rope, which was attached to a harness on a dark, four-legged creature. Though it had only been several hours since Landon had last seen him, it felt like it had been many years.

"Melech?" Landon said the word tentatively, in case it was only an apparition or a dream.

The horse bowed its regal head. "Young Landon."

Landon choked on a sob and ran to his friend. Melech became a blurred figure through Landon's tears, and then even blurrier as Landon wrapped his arms around Melech's neck and buried his face in his mane.

"I don't know what happened," said Landon. "It was like they took you away. . .from my mind." Landon lifted his head and stroked Melech's nose, sniffling. "But I missed you, still. I *missed* you."

Melech softly whinnied. It felt like a big cat's purr. "I missed you, too, young Landon. I feared I might not see you again. Forgive me for failing to save you from this spell."

"Forgive you? I'm the one who ignored the sign, the warnings. You should forgive *me.*"

The door to the tree remained open, and a figure appeared silhouetted against the amber light. It was Ludo.

"Ditty? Tardy Hardy? Second-to-None?" His voice rose in a whine. Suddenly he screamed. "Addlefoot! Battleroot! Scuddlebud! Man the casements! Shoot! Shoot! Shoot!"

Tardy Hardy was first on Melech's back. Then Ditty hopped aboard. They each grabbed one of Landon's hands and hoisted him up between them onto a blanketlike saddle. Melech wore a harness and bridle. Tardy Hardy undid a clip, and the rope he'd been holding fell away. Without warning, Melech reared up and pawed at the air, letting rip a tremulous neigh that would have struck fear into Landon's heart had it not been coming from his friend.

They came down with a thud, and Melech took off like a bolt. As the first arrows whistled past on either side, Landon felt an electric thrill surge through his body. Two delicate hands clasped his chest, and his heart beat even harder. Ditty's head pressed against his shoulder, and in her sweet, little voice, she asked, "Surprised?"

Landon wanted to laugh. "Yes." He was too overwhelmed and overjoyed to be riding Melech to know what else to say.

They approached two odd-looking bushes that appeared stuck together. As Melech hurtled over them, Landon heard the bushes moaning, making an "mmph-mmph" sound. He

glanced back to notice they weren't bushes after all, but two
Odds tied together, sitting back to back. They must have had
leaves in their mouths.

Landon felt Tardy Hardy's body jiggling. He was giggling.
Glancing over his shoulder, Tardy Hardy said, "Doze were
Wagglewhip and Trumplestump. Dey take horsy away. I take
horsy back but let dem keep nice new rope. Hee-hee. Whoa!"

The Odd lurched sideways as Melech veered right.
Landon saw his wide, goofy grin and could hear him giggling
again as he faced ahead.

"Where are we going?" Landon asked, turning to Ditty.
Three arrows sailed overhead, and Landon flinched. From the
corner of his eye he saw another one coming straight for them.

"Look out!" he cried, twisting his body around as far as
he could and trying to shove Ditty down. A piercing, ripping
sound came from behind him. Landon was afraid to look.
The Odd's giggling had abruptly stopped. *Oh no!*

"Oh no. Nuts and rats."

Landon turned. Tardy Hardy had his hand behind his
head, feeling the feathered shaft of the arrow that had gone
through the middle point of his cap. "Nutcrackers and
rattlesnakes," he said, lifting the hat from his head, inspecting
it, and then flinging it away.

Another arrow picked the hat from the air and nailed it to
a tree with a splintering sound. Tardy Hardy glanced back at
the tree with his mouth hanging open and his eyes wide with
alarm. He gave a single burst of laughter. "Hunh!" Then he said

thoughtfully, "Dey always did hate dat hat." He scratched his head through a mat of tousled hair and turned forward.

"So, where are we going?" Landon asked again. He was looking over one shoulder and then quickly switching to the other. Thankfully, the next several arrows missed by at least a foot in any given direction.

"We're going to Vates' place," said Ditty. "But first we have to get across the river."

Chapter Nineteen

By the time the three on horseback reached the mighty river, the arrows had finally ceased.

When Ditty had explained that in order to reach Vates' place, they first would have to cross the river, Landon hadn't given it much thought. But as he gazed from a high bank that sloped down to the water, Landon's heart sank. He was a fairly decent swimmer, but he wasn't *that* good.

Trying to squint through the misty darkness over the water, he could barely make out where the opposite bank began. And who knew what kinds of currents ran beneath the gently flowing surface? The idea of going into any water in the darkness gave Landon the willies.

"Get off here," Tardy Hardy said, "to gather stones."

Landon watched as the hatless Odd climbed down and then helped Ditty dismount. She looked at him. "Are you coming?"

Landon sighed. He could see his breath when he breathed deeply. "We're getting rocks to cross a river? What are we going to do, build a bridge? That'll take forever!"

Tardy Hardy had sauntered off into some tall grass and stooped over. He stood and pointed toward the edge of the water. "Da sign," he said. "Dat's why stones." He tilted his head. "Sorta build bridge. Sorta." He bent over and resumed rummaging through the grass.

The sign? All Landon could see was a faint silvery reflection on the water. Wait a second. There was something. A shadowy shape that was too distinct and sharp-edged to be natural. Landon climbed down. "You all right?" he asked, patting Melech's muscular neck. Melech didn't break his gaze from the river's vast expanse.

"Here, yes," said Melech, tamping the dirt with his hoof. "There, in that liquid, not so sure." He snorted, and a steamy cloud rose from his nostrils.

"Well, I'm going to check this out," said Landon. "I'm not too crazy about going in there, either." He was about to start down the bank, when he paused. "And Melech?"

The horse turned his head.

"I'm glad we're together again."

"Likewise, young Landon." Melech nodded, and Landon smiled.

There was indeed a sign jutting from the damp earth near the water, another wooden board on a post. The words on it were hard to make out in the dark. Then Landon remembered the firefly bubble in his boot.

It gave just the right amount of illumination, not too bright and not too dim. Holding the magically hovering bug before the board, Landon read the words:

LILY PAD CROSSING:
AVOID ATTEMPTING TO ENTER SWIMMING
MORE THAN A STONE'S THROW AWAY
MUCH MORE. . .

Lily pad crossing?

Landon held the light toward the river, but he couldn't see anything other than streaming water. As he glanced back at the sign, five letters seemed to jump out at him. The *V, A, T, E,* and *S* in the second line were darker than the other letters. "Vates," Landon whispered, shaking his head in wonder. He had to meet this mysterious sign-maker.

But first they had to cross the river, and still he had no idea how they could do it.

Ditty had joined Tardy Hardy in the grass. They each held the bottom hem of their shirt to form a pouch, and into the pouch they were dropping stones. *Yeah, that will help,* Landon thought sarcastically. They'd sink straight to the bottom!

Landon climbed the bank and watched them fill their shirts till they were bulging. "Have you *been* across the river?"

Ditty paused and shook her head. "I haven't, but he has." She pointed at Tardy Hardy as he came up with what appeared a sagging bellyful of rocks. The Odd grunted and swaggered from the grass toward Melech.

"Dis should be enough, with Ditty's," he said. He looked at Landon and waggled his head. "Help up?"

Landon interlaced his fingers like a stirrup and boosted Tardy Hardy up. He did the same for Ditty and then managed to clamber aboard and squeeze between them. A number of stones had spilled in the process, but no one seemed too concerned.

Melech took on the extra weight without complaint. He turned his head to address his passengers. "And now what are we to do?" he asked. His ears twitched in and out.

"Now we run cross to other side," said Tardy Hardy. "Look." He drew back a stone and pitched it toward the river. It splashed about ten feet out and disappeared without a trace.

Landon sighed. *Great.* Maybe Tardy Hardy really was as dense as he seemed. Landon was about to question this whole scheme when he noticed something taking shape in the river.

A gray circle had formed on the surface of the water where the stone had gone in. The circle continued to grow until it bumped against the shore. Then it began to shrink, and finally it was gone. The whole thing had taken less than ten seconds.

"What was that?" Landon asked, staring at the spot where the circle had been.

"Stone lily pad," said Tardy Hardy. "Way across."

Landon felt his mouth drop open. Behind him, he heard

Ditty say, "This should be fun!" It was a long way to the other side, and suddenly Landon wondered about those spilled rocks. He was about to ask if he should go get some more, when Tardy Hardy bounced on the saddle and said, "Giddap, horsy! Giddap!"

Landon forced his eyes open as they lurched down the bank. Tardy Hardy's arm worked in a frenzy, tossing out stones one after another. *Splish! Splish! Splish!* Little fountains burst before them, and the soft thudding of Melech's hooves became a sharp clattering as they crossed the first circle of stone.

But Tardy Hardy seemed to be throwing more than Melech could keep up with. And Landon felt sure he had seen a few handfuls of stones thrown out, wasting many, rather than only one at a time. Nervously, Landon tapped the Odd's shoulder. "Slow down," Landon said. "We're not even halfway across yet."

Tardy Hardy threw both his hands in the air, and Landon gasped.

"I'm out! I'm out! I'm out!" the Odd shouted. "No more stones! Doomed! Ditty, help!"

"He's out?" Ditty cried. "What happened?" But before she had finished her question she was already pitching her first stone. After getting cuffed on his left shoulder—twice— Landon figured out she was a lefty, so he leaned to his right to give her more room to throw.

Ditty wasn't as quick as Tardy Hardy, which was a good thing. But it meant Melech had to start jumping from one stone pad to the next. He was racing like a champion steeplechaser. Every now and then a hoof would catch the edge of the stone and make a splash. The extra distance Melech was making up in the air wasn't going to be enough, however. In a panicky voice, Ditty cried, "I'm almost out, too! Just a few stones left!"

Landon squinted against the mist. The once-distant bank was getting close but not close enough. If only he had collected some stones! Landon reached for the one thing he had. Plucking the lightning bug bubble from his boot, he held it out at the ready. When Ditty said, "That's it! They're gone!" Landon threw the little sphere as hard as he could. He watched in horror as the light landed on the water, floated like a bobber, and drifted away downstream.

"No!" Landon cried. Feeling sick to his stomach, he braced himself for the icy water. But it never came.

Perhaps it was the sight of the approaching shore, or the sense that no more stone lily pads were forthcoming, or his exceptional fear of the water. One or all of those elements combined with Melech's hindquarters to produce an explosion of power that launched them into the air in a soaring arc. Their cries of "whee-hee-hee," "whoaaa," "aaahhh," and "eee" created a cacophony of sound that ended abruptly when Melech's hooves touched the ground and all three passengers' jaws clamped shut. *Ba-dump!*

They ascended the bank. Landon saw stars and then tree-tops. They were on the other side. They had crossed the river.

Melech slowed at the top of the bank and turned back.

Landon stared across the expanse of the river. No signs remained of any stone lily pads. It was too far to see the posted board with Vates' message.

"Avoid attempting to enter swimming," Landon said quietly. "We did it." He realized, of course, that all he had done was throw a perfectly good firefly ball into the river, but he didn't mention that. He imagined it was probably halfway to the ocean by now.

Ditty leaned around Landon and poked Tardy Hardy in the back. "I thought you said you'd crossed before."

Tardy Hardy shrugged at her touch and lowered his head. "Did," he said. "Did cross."

"How'd you do it?" asked Ditty. "We barely made it with a horse."

"Didn't *enter* swimming," said Tardy Hardy, "but did exit dat way."

Ditty sighed, and then she giggled. "Whew! I'm glad we don't have to do that again. Though it was kind of fun."

Landon's whole body felt wet and chilled. The dampness was partly from the mist, but also, he realized, from his own perspiration.

He thought about what Ditty had said. Wasn't she planning to go back? Was she running away from Ludo and the Echoing Green permanently? He could understand not wanting to return. Still, the thought of never going home made him sad.

Home. His family. Grandpa Karl. Landon sighed.

"Is something wrong?" Ditty asked, touching his arm.

Landon almost started. "Oh," he said, "I was just thinking about my family. About, well. . .I'm not sure how to get home."

Melech turned from the river and carried them into the forest. The dry, woodsy air smelled good and felt good, too. Landon let out a shiver that had built up from the run across the river. If he ever did make it home, would he have some stories to share!

They sauntered at an easy pace through the trees, enjoying the quiet of the night and the lack of flying arrows. Landon asked about the animals that Ditty had said once filled the forest. She explained that the shadows had come and changed everything. Especially Ludo. He commanded that all animals be taken someplace beyond the valley, never to "infect" the forest again. When Landon asked why, Ditty said, "The animals made us happy. They were taken away to make us forget when all was right in the valley."

Landon sensed there was much more to the story, but it seemed to make Ditty sad talking about it, so he quit asking questions.

The darkness shifted toward gray twilight, and Melech paused, raising his head and pricking up his ears. "There it is again, young Landon," Melech said. "Ohhh-whoa. A thousand voices."

"Uh-oh," said Tardy Hardy. "Dat's da Coin toss, and I'm late. . .again." He turned with a big, wide grin. "Master Ludo won't be happy about dat." An expression of mock gravity puckered his face.

At the sound of Ditty giggling, a warm feeling of relief and friendship spread through Landon's body. His happiness was tinged by loneliness—an achy longing for home.

A rosy glow began to trickle through the treetops. Melech moved on, and Landon breathed in the fresh morning air. For a while they swayed in a quietness broken only by the crunching of Melech's hooves upon the forest floor and the occasional soft pat of dew upon a leaf.

Suddenly Melech stopped. They all seemed to strain their ears toward a distant whistle of two notes: one high note followed quickly by a lower tone.

Twee-too.

Twee-too.

Landon's heart leapt at the sound. Closing his eyes a moment, he imagined a single bird calling from a solitary branch.

Twee-too.

Twee-too.

The forest resonated with those two notes.

The growing brightness of the leaves seemed to come from the birdsong as much as from the stretching fingers of sunlight. Landon thought perhaps not only he, but Tardy Hardy and Ditty and even Melech were being called home somehow.

Melech began to trot and then to gallop. By the time they reached the edge of the forest, Landon felt streams of tears flying back from the corners of his eyes. He wasn't feeling sad. Something curious and unexpected was flooding his soul. The anticipation of joy.

The mountains appeared at once close and far away, like a purplish mural painted against the sky. Before the mountains rose the foothills, some covered by trees, some mere grassy knolls, and some with patches of both. As Landon and his friends approached the first hill, three strange things came to his attention. First, the hill had an inset oval window with crisscrossed lines running through it. Second, next to the window, a framework of cut logs arched over a doorway. And third, a faint wisp of smoke was rising from the top of the hill.

A small grove of trees stood off to the right, somehow distinct from the vast forest of the valley. Landon was about to dismount and go knock on the door, when a voice came from the direction of the grove.

Chapter Twenty

Sound the trumpets and pass the tea and crumplets! I have visitors. Ha!"

An old man with a white beard emerged from the trees waving a stick. He stopped abruptly with the stick in midair, pivoted around, and went back among the trees. A moment later, he reappeared, tucking a scroll beneath one arm and jabbing the stick into the ground to pull himself along. He stepped right to them, looking at Melech, Tardy Hardy, Landon, Ditty, and then back to Landon.

"It is good to see you. I'm glad you made it. Please, come on in." He turned toward the hill, propelling his slightly hunched form almost as if through a bog. "Don't worry about your footgear," he called over his shoulder, "drag in as much dirt as you want!"

The three riders climbed down and followed the old man

to the door. On the way, Landon tapped Tardy Hardy. "Is that Vates?" he whispered.

The old man swung about. "Of course I am!" he said. "Who else would live out here like this? Some crazy hermit?" His scowl melted into a smile, and he looked past Landon and waggled his stick. "You, too," he said, apparently addressing Melech. "I've got apples and water and maybe a sugar lump, but it's all inside. So come on."

Vates pushed the latchless wood door and held it as they filed in. When Melech had entered, barely scraping through the doorway, Vates released the door and it sprang shut, pausing at the last instant before quietly closing.

The room was earthy and dusty and filled with bookshelves, which in turn were full of books. Sunlight streamed in through the window, creating a warm, bright atmosphere despite the dingy corners. Vates stepped through to another doorway that led to another room. "I suppose you three are tired of sitting, while Mr. Horse here—"

"Melech, if you please, sir," said Melech, bowing his head. Landon felt a rush of pride.

"While Mr. Melech has been on his hooves all day. Still, I can only offer the three of you places to sit, and you, Melech, a place to stand." Vates half shrugged as he gestured toward four rough wooden chairs at a rugged wooden table. Two of the chairs as well as most of the table were covered with books.

"Be right back," said Vates. "Please make yourselves at home." He disappeared into the other room.

Landon looked at his friends. Tardy Hardy stared after Vates, a trickle of drool forming at the corner of his open mouth. Ditty was gaping at the books, her big eyes rising and falling among the shelves.

She glanced at Landon. "Can he read all these, do you think?"

"I'm sure he can," said Landon. "If you can read one book, well, you can usually read a lot of others."

"I'd like to read a book," she said. She looked as hungry to read as Tardy Hardy did to eat, although she didn't drool about it.

Melech was looking at Landon, and when Landon caught his eye, he glanced away. A gentle snort emitted from Melech's flared nostrils. The horse seemed to be sensing what Landon was feeling—that he was going to leave this place soon and before that he would be saying good-bye. Landon just didn't know when or, more important, how he would go about leaving and getting home.

"Well, I see you're all still standing. Please. . .seats. . . chairs. . .oh, excuse the books."

Vates set a tray on the corner of the table and cleared off the two chairs with books. Landon sat down, and Ditty and Tardy Hardy followed suit.

Vates served each of them a steaming mug of cinnamon tea and offered a plate with apple slices and things that looked like biscuits. To Melech, Vates brought a small bucket and another plate of apples and—

"Crumplets," said Vates, joining the threesome at the table. "A combination of cookie, crumpet, and biscuit. I'm fairly proud of them, though this batch turned out a bit dry, not sure why." He took a bite and made a face, nodding. "Yup. Dry. Ah, well. Go ahead and dip them if you'd like."

He dunked the crumplet into his mug and chewed, raising his eyebrows. "Mm-hmm. Much better. Now, Hardy, when you finish that mouthful, and that one, and—Hardy, slow down. I'd like you to introduce me to your friends. Now, I've already met Mr. Melech, there. . ."

Landon reached out his hand. "I'm Landon Snow, sir."

Vates smiled and lowered his eyebrows. He seemed to look at Landon and through him at the same time. Though Vates' skin was weathered and wrinkled, his eyes sparkled with an ageless gleam. "Landon Snow." He took Landon's hand and held it between his. "It is so good to know you."

Landon had the feeling that Vates really did know him more than was possible from their brief meeting. Somehow, this didn't seem strange. Vates seemed a man who knew a lot of things—and not just from his books.

Tardy Hardy gulped and belched and licked his lips. "And dis is Ditty," he said gesturing toward her with one hand while grabbing two crumplets with the other.

Vates smiled at her, and they shook hands. "I've heard about you, you know," said Vates. "You sound like quite a girl, Ditty."

Her eyes grew big, and she smiled, even as she seemed to shrink in shy sheepishness. "Thank you, Mr. Vates."

"How do you know Tardy Hardy?" Landon asked. Then he thought to rephrase it toward Tardy Hardy. "How do you know Mr. Vates?"

Tardy Hardy's eyes bulged as his lips and cheeks undulated vigorously. "Mmnph mmnph mmnph *mmnph*." He smiled, keeping his mouth closed, thank goodness.

"Please," said Vates, gesturing toward himself. "I'm Vates, plain and simple. No 'sir' or 'mister' necessary. And my friend Hardy is just plain Hardy. He's only tardy in the minds of certain Odds and a fellow named Ludo. And the reason he's tardy is because he's been running errands for me."

"Errands?" asked Landon.

"Posting signs and such. You don't think I go running back and forth with those things, do you?" He smiled and then glanced at Hardy. "And you arrived damp-free and with an appetite greater than your thirst, for once. Thanks to our friend, Mr. Melech, I presume."

"Mmnph." Hardy nodded and pointed at Melech. "Mmm-hmmph."

Vates took a sip from his mug. The food and drink looked and smelled good, but for some reason, Landon couldn't get himself to partake.

"Well," said Vates, setting down his mug. "Landon Snow. Are you ready?"

Did he know the way for Landon to get home? Landon glanced around, feeling anxious and excited. One tall bookshelf stood backed against the wall. . . .

He looked at Vates and felt his heart beginning to hammer. Landon took a deep breath and slowly nodded. "Yes," he said in a hoarse whisper.

"Good," said Vates. "Then let's get started. Do you remember the first part?"

The first part? Landon looked at the table as the hammering in his chest dropped to a slow bounce. "The first part of what?" He glanced up uncertainly.

Vates leaned forward. "The Auctor's Riddle, of course. I do hope that's what you came here to solve." It sounded sort of like a question.

"Ohhh," said Landon, sliding his gaze toward the window. "Yes."

"Is that your answer to the first part, or are you saying you do remember it?"

"I remember," said Landon, meeting Vates' eyes. "I do remember it."

Vates leaned back and sighed. "Well, let's hear it then." He closed his eyes intensely, waiting.

"Could it be chance, mere circumstance, that man eats cow eats grass eats soil, and then man dies, and when he lies, to soil he does return?"

Vates had been subtly nodding along, as if waiting for a slip or incorrect word. When Landon finished, the old man's face relaxed. He opened his eyes. "Very good," he said, and Landon couldn't help but beam. "So, what is your reply to part one?"

Landon looked at the table and traced the arc of the

handle on his mug. He could smell the cinnamon. "I don't think so," he said finally. "It's too perfect to be an accident or to happen by chance."

Vates nodded. "I see. And what do you think of part two, then. Do you remember it?"

Landon stopped tracing the handle, and he drew his hand away. "No," he said. "I don't. I can't remember it." He looked at Ditty. "I only saw it once, and—"

"Here." Ditty held something out to him that she must have had in a pocket somewhere. It was a flimsy, filmy piece of paper almost like sheer cloth. "I had written it down before you came."

Landon's mouth fell open. "I thought you couldn't read? How did you—"

Her gaze fell slightly, and she shook her head. "I can't, I can't read. I just copied the lines and shapes—the letters, right?—like how they were on the sign." She glanced shyly between Landon and Vates.

Vates reached out and took the piece of cloth-paper. He unfolded it and held it tenderly, studying it. One of his eyebrows rose and so did half of his mouth. "Well, this is most extraordinary, Ditty. This is most extraordinary."

She smiled and seemed to blush, although her skin color didn't really change.

"And I thought Ludo had confiscated and burned most extraneous writing materials. Hmmm." Vates handed the paper to Landon.

The writing was very scratchy and rudimentary, but he could make out the letters and words soon enough.

"Could it be chance. . .coincidence? That sun turns earth turns moon turns seas. And so there are years, and sally—no, *salty*—*beach tears. So. . .ticks. . .celestial. . .time."*

"So, what do you think?" Vates asked.

"Is this talking about gravity?" asked Landon. Vates nodded. "And like, the orbits of the moon around the earth and the earth around the sun?" Another nod. "What are salty beach tears?" Landon asked.

"The tides, more or less, saltwater, also affected by gravity—the earth's and the moon's pull."

"And all that happening by coincidence?" said Landon. He shook his head. "It doesn't really seem possible, does it? Again, it just seems too. . .neat. I don't know."

Vates stood and went to the front door where, on a shelf, he had set the scroll he'd had tucked beneath his arm when they had come in. He came back, shoved some of the books aside on the table, removed the tray—which Hardy took from him and held—and set down the scroll. Unrolling it toward Landon, Vates said, "And now I present to you Part Three of the Auctor's Riddle."

Landon recognized the script and looked up at Vates, who gave him a wink. "Go ahead," said Vates, "for all to hear."

Landon cleared his throat. "Ahem." As soon as he started to read, however, his throat began to strangely constrict. It wasn't as if someone was choking him. Rather, it was as if he was suddenly overcome by another presence in the room. A presence that was cloaking him. A presence that had been with him all along his fantastic journey. A presence that Landon somehow knew was the Presence of the Auctor himself.

Landon cleared his throat again for real. He wiped his eyes with his sleeve and started over, using all his strength and concentration to make it through to the end:

> *Or might there be one, above creation*
> *Who designed and created and shaped and colored*
> *Who put where they are, the earth, moon, and star*
> *And a boy named Landon Snow to wonder. . .in awe.*

He hadn't quite made it, however. When he read his own name, he had to choke back a sob. It seemed silly, really. Landon didn't know why he was reacting so emotionally. It was only a riddle, right? Right? He found himself nodding.

"Is that your response? Are you okay, Landon Snow?"

Landon wiped his eyes again and smiled at Vates. A sound came up through his throat that was like a laugh and a sob all at once. "Yeah," Landon said, "I'm okay. And I know who the Auctor is. He's the Author of everything. He's God, isn't he?"

Vates closed his eyes and bowed his head. "The answers are so simple. The implications so enormous. You have answered well, Landon Snow. And I hope you always remember. Not necessarily the riddle. Not necessarily the answers to the riddle. But the Auctor of this crazy riddle we call life."

Chapter Twenty-One

Before Landon said good-bye to his friends, he had to ask Vates something. "Will I. . .I mean, can I come back here. . .again?"

"Would you like to?"

Landon looked at Hardy, Ditty, and Melech. "Yes."

"Then I suppose it might well be possible. Your first visit has certainly benefited some." Vates paused as Ditty loudly sniffed and Melech swished his tail and softly neighed. Hardy belched and grinned.

Landon wanted to ask how he might come back, and he furtively turned to peek at the bookcase near the wall. One last question came to mind. "Vates?" he asked.

Vates had rolled up the scroll of Part Three and was setting it across two stacks of books. He really was not a good housekeeper, for all his apparent wisdom.

"Yes?" Vates said. "I am listening."

"How did you erase Bart's gravestone and write the first part of the riddle there?"

Vates' eyes twinkled brightly. "Ah. Well, you see, for me that would be very tricky, very tricky indeed. But nothing is impossible for the Auctor. Even things that are apparently written in stone. Besides, the engraving is on a stone book, is it not? And you well know, Landon Snow, that a book always has more than one page."

Landon frowned, but Vates' smiling eyes proved too much. He wasn't going to give a straightforward answer, apparently. Landon laughed. "A book of stone. Turn the page. Right."

Landon said good-bye to Hardy first, mussing the Odd's already messy hair. "Thanks," Landon said. "For catching me and especially for getting Melech back." Hardy looked at him steadily, and then, catching Landon off guard, he gave that fast-twitching wink.

Ditty stood and hugged Landon, taking his breath away. "I'll miss you," she said. Landon's face was burning and his heart thumping. "Me, too," he managed to get out softly. "Thanks for breaking the spell on me."

Ditty stepped back and looked at him, her wide eyes unblinking. "Anytime," she said, reaching out to give him two quick taps on the nose.

Melech lifted his head and pricked up his ears. Landon stroked his neck and ran his fingers through his black mane. "I have done my duty, young Landon, and—"

"I know, Melech, I know. You're glad for it, and so am I."

Melech turned his head to look at Landon. "And now it is time for you to do yours. You may step off here at the corner. I think you will be all right."

Landon nodded, partly to hide his suddenly trembling lip. He buried his face in Melech's neck and hugged him as tightly as when they'd gone zigzagging down the slope toward the cliff.

"You're the best friend I've ever had," said Landon, sniffling.

He felt Melech's muscles ripple as he gave a gentle neigh. "As you are mine, young Landon, as you are mine. Now carry on and fare thee well."

Landon smiled and sniffed. Both of his sleeves were damp from wiping. Taking a deep breath, he began walking toward the bookcase. "I'm ready now," he said to Vates, who remained near the table.

"Then why are you going over there?" asked Vates. "The only way out is the same way you came in." He gestured with his head toward the door.

Landon pointed at the bookshelf. "The way I came in was, well, originally. . ."

Vates took two steps toward the front door. "There's nothing back there but earthen wall, I'm afraid. And I don't have the strength to move that shelf."

Perplexed, Landon turned around and walked to the door. Vates opened it and held it for him. Placing a hand on Landon's shoulder, he said, "You will remember, right?"

"The Auctor," said Landon. "I won't forget him."

"And one more thing: remember that life is an open-book riddle. I'm glad you came, Landon. Good-bye."

"Good-bye, Vates," said Landon.

The next thing he knew, he was standing outside in the shade, hearing the spring-loaded door pause and then ease shut behind him.

Over his head hung a ceiling of white planks. Beyond the ceiling, sunshine glared. Landon was standing on a platform of some sort with a short series of steps before him. On either side was a rail supported by many posts. Beyond the rail extended a yard and then some trees. Everything looked so strange and yet so familiar. Landon slowly looked to his left, and a woozy feeling came over him.

He was looking at a long gravel driveway in which sat a maroon sedan. It was his father's car.

Landon felt his clothing and looked at himself. He was barefoot and wearing striped pajamas. A shudder ran up his spine both from the chilly air and the discombobulation. He knew where he was, of course, and yet he couldn't quite believe it. "Vates?" he said tentatively. "How did I—"

A noise sounded behind him. Landon turned to see through a screen to another solid door that was opening. An old man appeared wearing a gray beard and spectacles. He struggled with the screened door, seemingly oblivious to Landon. Finally Landon reached out and opened the door, and the old man jumped.

"Landon? What on earth are you doing out here? I

thought you'd still be sleeping."

Landon worked his mouth and tongue, trying to find the right words. He knew they were in there somewhere. Finally, out they came. "Grandpa Karl? What happened?"

"Oh." Grandpa Karl held up two white oven mitts, one on each hand. But then he wiggled his exposed thumbs. "They wrapped them up at the hospital. I'll be part mummy for a couple weeks, I guess." He rolled his eyes. "Stupid jalopy. Come on in—oh, could you fetch that paper there?"

Landon retrieved a folded newspaper from the bottom porch step and went inside. Warm and wonderful smells greeted him. "Breakfast is about ready," said Grandpa Karl. "And looky there, your sisters are up, too."

"Grandpa!" Bridget started to run but then stopped, stretched, and yawned. She resumed her advance toward her grandfather more slowly. Grandpa Karl reached around her, and she said, "What's wrong with your hands?"

"Oh, I had an accident last night." He sighed. "Looks like your dad's going to have to shuttle us all back and forth to the BUL today. That is, if you kids still want to go."

"I want to go," said Holly. She had on a long flannel night-gown. "And I'm taking my calculator this time and a notebook."

"Breakfast, breakfast!" Grandma Alice called from the kitchen. "Come and get it."

Landon's mom was carrying a bowl of steaming scrambled eggs to the table. His dad was sipping a cup of coffee, his eyes half drooping.

"Hey, birthday boy," said his dad. "So how's it feel to be eleven these days?" He smiled wearily.

"You look tired, Dad," said Landon. It really felt like he was walking through a dream.

"Yeah, I don't seem to have the stamina your grandfather has. Must have skipped a generation." He slurped his coffee and set down the cup.

They gathered around the table, and Landon's dad slowly stood. They bowed their heads, and Grandpa Karl prayed, especially thanking God for Landon on his birthday. When they all said, "Amen," Landon almost said, "Auctor." He smiled to himself.

Holly shared that she'd counted 230 sheep before falling asleep. Bridget yawned and said she'd only seen one sheep, and he didn't make it over the fence. Everyone laughed.

"And how about you, Landon?" Grandma Alice asked. "Any adventures for you last night? Well," she added, "after your grandfather's little mishap."

Grandpa Karl was having a hard time getting any eggs to stay on his fork. He finally settled for nibbling some bacon and toast, which he could grasp easily enough.

"Well," said Landon. "I didn't see any sheep. But I did go down to the library."

Grandpa Karl nodded approvingly. Landon's mom said, "You mean you dreamed you were in the library?"

How do you like your eggs? Landon thought. *Scrambled? What about sunny side up, me friend?*

A smile played at the corner of Landon's lips. Then he

almost gasped. His dream-stone. . .it was still in Bart's cabin at the library. Wasn't it?

"Landon? Are you still dreaming?"

His sisters were giggling. Landon thought of Ditty and smiled.

"My dream—yeah, it's in the library. I mean, I'm looking forward to going back there."

"How about after a nap?" suggested his dad. "That midnight run to Brainerd did me in."

"Sounds good to me," said Grandpa Karl, waving his bandaged hands. "The BUL doesn't open till ten anyway."

Landon downed his juice and said, "If you'll excuse me, please?"

His grandparents nodded. Grandma Alice said, "Why certainly. It's your birthday! You can do what you want. There are more lemon bars for later." She smiled.

"Thanks," said Landon. He walked down the hallway to Grandpa Karl's study. The door was closed, and he hesitated. Would the bookcase still be open? He turned the doorknob and looked inside. The shade was still drawn so the room had an amber glow. With some disappointment, he noticed the bookcase was pressed flush against the wall.

His Bible—Bartholomew G. Benneford's old book—lay open on the desk with the drawing Landon had made for his grandparents. Well, it was really for Grandpa Karl, since he was in it. Landon looked at it and cringed. He was a terrible artist.

The dream-stone was missing. It was not on the drawing, or behind the typewriter, or on the floor, or on the sofa bed.

It wasn't anywhere. Landon's heart skipped a beat. It had happened. Hadn't it?

The Bible was open to the book of Acts. A few lines had been neatly underscored by one of the previous owners, though Landon was sure old Bart was responsible. The passage was Acts 2:17: "And it shall come to pass in the last days, saith God, I will pour out of my Spirit upon all flesh: and your sons and daughters shall prophesy, and your young men shall see visions, and your old men shall dream dreams."

The pages started turning, flipping from left to right. Landon took a step back and watched, scarcely breathing. The fluttering continued until hardly any pages were left to turn. When the final one floated down, Landon stepped forward and looked. It was open to Genesis, the first book of the Bible. The first verse had been underlined, again with that straight, neat pen. Inside his head, Landon heard Vates' voice as he had stepping through the doorway: *"And one more thing, remember that life is an open-book riddle."*

Landon read the open book: "In the beginning God created the heaven and the earth."

Landon looked up and smiled. He looked all the way up to the ceiling, but that's not where he was looking. "I know," Landon said. "Thanks for the reminder."

His night of adventures caught up with him, and Landon felt very tired. So he lay down on his open sleeping bag and fell into a dreamless sleep. Upstairs his dad was napping while Grandpa Karl leaned back in his easy chair near the fireplace and began to snore. Bridget dozed on the sofa while Holly counted teacups and saucers and tiny spoons in Grandma Alice's extensive collection. Grandma Alice puttered in the kitchen and smiled at Holly. Landon's mom found a quiet corner to read a chapter in a novel and work on the crossword puzzle in the newspaper.

When Landon awoke he felt refreshed, and soon everyone was gathered for the trek to the BUL. When they reached the stairs, Landon had a hard time restraining himself from racing into the building. Unable to hold back any longer, he ran up the final steps, past the rowboat tombstone in the foyer and into Bart's Reading Room, the old log cabin in the corner.

The rugged reading chair stood in the middle of the room. Landon glanced to his right at the bookcase, which was now snug against the wall. Guessing at the stone's trajectory from his lobbing it up the stairway, he traced an invisible path through the air, onto the floor, and over to the opposite wall. He could scarcely breathe, he was so anxious. Had it all been a strange and wonderful dream? Or was it real? Walking along the wood planks toward the left wall, Landon's heart pounded with hope. *Please be here,* he thought. *Please be here!*

The egg-shaped stone was resting near the wall face up, waiting. Landon nearly trembled with happiness and excitement as he crouched to pick it up. He read aloud the engraved word, "Dream," and smiled. Feeling the stone's heft and hard cool smoothness, Landon stepped back out to the foyer. He paused to look up at the brilliant chandelier, and then marched on to join his family on their way to the main collection room. One thing was certain, thought Landon. The library sure did look a lot different in the daytime.

Be Sure to Watch for:

Landon Snow

and the Shadows of
Malus Quidam

Coming Spring 2006!